by Henry Winkler and Lin Oliver

HANK ZIPZER

The World's Greatest Underachiever

My Dog's a Scaredy-Cat

Grosset & Dunlap

To all the children who work so hard to shake hands with their learning challenges, I salute you. And as always, to Stacey.—H.W.

For Lynne and Alex, with happy memories of all those Halloweens.—L.O.

Cover illustration by Jesse Joshua Watson

GROSSET & DUNLAP
Published by the Penguin Group
Penguin Group (USA) Inc., 375 Hudson Street, New York, New York 10014, U.S.A.
Penguin Group (Canada), 90 Eglinton Avenue East, Suite 700,
Toronto, Ontario, Canada M4P 2Y3
(a division of Pearson Penguin Canada Inc.)
Penguin Books Ltd, 80 Strand, London WC2R 0RL, England
Penguin Ireland, 25 St Stephen's Green, Dublin 2, Ireland
(a division of Penguin Books Ltd)
Penguin Group (Australia), 250 Camberwell Road, Camberwell,
Victoria 3124, Australia (a division of Pearson Australia Group Pty Ltd)
Penguin Books India Pvt Ltd, 11 Community Centre,
Panchsheel Park, New Delhi - 110 017, India
Penguin Group (NZ), Cnr Airborne and Rosedale Roads,
Albany, Auckland 1310, New Zealand (a division of Pearson New Zealand Ltd)
Penguin Books (South Africa) (Pty) Ltd, 24 Sturdee Avenue,
Rosebank, Johannesburg 2196, South Africa

Penguin Books Ltd, Registered Offices:
80 Strand, London WC2R 0RL, England

Library of Congress Control Number: 2006004898

ISBN 0-448-43878-X (pbk)   10 9
ISBN 0-448-43879-8 (hc)   10 9 8 7 6 5 4 3

Special Markets ISBN 0-448-44522-0 Not for resale

CHAPTER 1

"YOU'RE GOING AS A *WHAT*?" Frankie Townsend, my best friend, practically screamed at me.

"I'm telling you, Frankie," I shot back. "No one has ever had this idea for a Halloween costume before."

"That's because no one is as insane as you are, Zip."

I had called Frankie and Ashley and told them they had to hurry to our clubhouse for a special meeting to discuss my brilliant idea for a Halloween costume. Ashley hadn't arrived yet, but I was so pumped up that I couldn't wait, so I just blurted my idea out to Frankie. It was not hard to notice that he didn't seem to think my idea was as brilliant as I did. As a matter of fact, I noticed that he thought it was totally stupid. And insane. And dangerous, too.

Usually, Frankie and I agree on most everything. Like the fact that our teacher Ms. Adolf is the worst teacher in the world. Like the fact that *The Moth That Ate Toledo* is as excellent an example of moviemaking as you could ever hope to find. Like the fact that boxers are better than briefs, and that your feet should never be tucked in tight when you're in bed. We think it sucks having the sheets so tight that they squish your toes under your feet like you're some kind of three-toed sloth.

So you can probably see why I was shocked that Frankie didn't like my idea for a Halloween costume.

"Frankie, the trouble with you is that you don't have an imagination with personality," I told him.

"Hank, the trouble with you is that you have an imagination that is totally freaky."

"What is wrong with going as a table in an Italian restaurant?" I demanded to know. "Tell me in twenty-five words or less."

"I can tell you in one word, Zip. E-v-e-r-y-t-h-i-n-g."

"Are you seriously telling me that my idea isn't clever and original?"

"I'm telling you that you're going to be laughed out of the school yard, if not pushed."

I flopped down on the beat-up purple-flowered couch and sighed. Then I coughed, because when you flop down on that couch, a huge cloud of dust erupts from the pillows like a volcano. Our clubhouse is in the basement of our apartment building, just down the hall from the laundry room. The clubhouse is really supposed to be a storage room where people keep things they don't use every day, like Christmas decorations or a bicycle with a flat tire. Mrs. Park, who lives on the seventh floor, put the flowered couch there last year when she got a new brown velvet one. There's a lot of dust that's collected in its pillows since then, but we don't care. I mean, how many kids do you know who have a clubhouse that comes complete with its own purple-flowered couch?

I put my feet up on the big iron birdcage that Mr. Grasso kept his pet parrot in before it flew away. Mr. Grasso told us that he named his parrot Gershwin because the bird liked to sing old Broadway tunes written by this guy named George Gershwin and his brother, Ira. That's a funny name, Ira. It sounds like it should be the name of a government office building, like: "The Ira Building will be closed on Saturdays and public holidays."

I hope Gershwin is living in Central Park now, with some bird friends who like to sing, too.

"Zip," Frankie said, snapping his fingers in front of me. "Where are you, man?"

"I was in Central Park, but I'm back now," I said.

My mind wanders a lot, but Frankie is used to that. You get used to everything about each other when you've been best friends your whole lives.

"Hey, guys. I came as soon as dinner was over."

It was Ashley Wong, our other best friend, who lives on the fourth floor of our building. She was breathing hard as she rounded the corner into the clubhouse, so she must have run down the stairs instead of taking the elevator.

"What's the urgent meeting about?" she asked me. "Another Hank Zipzer brainstorm?"

"Hank wants to discuss his idea for the

Halloween costume he's going to wear in the school parade tomorrow," Frankie said. "Hank, my man, go ahead. Tell Ashweena what you've decided to go as."

"I can't believe it," I said to Ashley. "Frankie's got a problem with the fact that I'm going as a table in an Italian restaurant."

"That's amazing," Ashley said, "because I'm going as a bowl of pasta in white clam sauce."

"You're kidding," I said.

"Yes, I am," she snapped back. "And I hope you are, too. Tell me you're not serious, Hank."

"What is wrong with you two?" I asked. "Does everyone have to go as some kind of bloodsucking vampire? That's so third grade."

Frankie came over and flopped down next to me.

"Hank, let me tell you how it is," he said, coughing from the dust his butt had kicked up. He put his hand on my shoulder and got that look on his face that he gets when he's explaining complicated things to me, like the plot of *The Moth That Ate Toledo (Part Two)* or how you figure out the earned run average of a pitcher. He looked me right in the eye.

"Hear me, dude. Blood is Halloween. Fangs are Halloween. Oozing scars and a rubber nail stuck in your cheek are Halloween. A table in an Italian restaurant is so not Halloween. It's not even Easter."

"Hank," Ashley chimed in. "It's our duty as your friends to warn you that if you go in the costume you're thinking of, everybody in the entire fifth grade will be talking about you. And you won't like what they're saying."

"Fine, you've warned me," I said. "But when you see me tomorrow in a red-and-white checkered tablecloth, with breadsticks in one hand and garlic-scented olive oil in the other, your minds will be changed forever."

"Did he just say garlic-scented olive oil?" Frankie asked Ashley.

"Yes, I'm pretty sure he did." She nodded.

"Ashweena, that tells me that this is way more than we can deal with. Way more."

"I can pull this off, guys," I said. "I don't want to be just another mummy. I want to express myself. Be creative."

"Will you consider a bribe?" Ashley said.

"I'll buy you two slices of pepperoni pizza if you change your mind."

I shook my head.

"Not even for a whole pizza with sausage, Canadian bacon, pineapple, and extra cheese," I said.

Frankie got up and headed for the door, stepping over Gershwin's cage and a box of Mrs. Fink's old baking pans. Mrs. Fink lives next door to us, and she makes the best cherry strudel in the world. If you ever run in to her, you have got to ask her for a piece. Put some vanilla ice cream on top, eat that puppy up, and you'll be smiling for a week. I'm not kidding.

"Hankster, we tried to warn you, but we failed," Frankie said. "So good luck. And when you come home tomorrow after the parade and crawl under your bed for the next six months, don't forget to send me a postcard."

"You'll see," I said to Frankie and Ashley. "I'm going to win first prize for originality. And by the way, I'll be accepting all apologies tomorrow in the clubhouse between the hours of four and six-thirty."

Boy, I hoped I was right. I was sure my

costume was going to be brilliant.

    I had to be right.

    I'm absolutely right.

    Right???

CHAPTER 2

As I rode up in the elevator to the tenth floor, I could hardly stand still. Now, that's not so unusual for me, because I have learning differences. Dr. Berger, who is my educational therapist at school, says that lots of kids with learning challenges are in constant motion. Sometimes I'm just sitting in school and I look down and notice that my leg is bouncing up and down a mile a minute.

But that night, I knew that my bouncing around in the elevator wasn't from my learning challenges. It was from being both very excited and very nervous about turning myself into a walking Italian table.

Ashley and Frankie had given me some pretty strong warnings, which I have to confess, were making my stomach do a few double backflips. But I have the kind of personality that when someone tells me *not* to do something, I want to do it even more. My mom calls it a stubborn streak. Talking to Ashley and Frankie got my stubborn streak all fired up and made me determined to become a table in an Italian restaurant.

As I got closer to our floor, I noticed that thoughts were flashing through my mind faster than the numbers flashing above the elevator door. It's cool when I have an idea that I think nobody's ever had before. It makes my brain all busy and full of thoughts, like the way the very first caveguy who discovered fire must have felt.

Wait! What if the caveman was a cavewoman? Who said it had to be a caveguy? Well, whoever it was, I'll bet he or she felt really great about it.

I couldn't wait to get started building my costume. As I got out of the elevator, I made a mental list of what I would need. I'd start with my mom's old red-and-white checkered tablecloth and cut a hole in the middle for my head to slip through. I'd need cardboard to make a square tabletop. I'd cut a hole in the cardboard and slip that over my shoulders before I put the tablecloth on.

Mental note to self. Don't use a cardboard box that our dog Cheerio pooped in.

Then I'd need to put some things on the table-top. Things you'd find in an Italian restaurant. Like a glass filled with breadsticks. And maybe a candle stuck in an old bottle.

Mental note to self. Don't light candle. It would be a drag to set off a fire alarm in the middle of the Halloween parade.

Then I had what I considered to be my most brilliant idea yet. I could make a chair out of cardboard and tape it to my butt.

Mental note to self. Use lots of tape to cover butt region so chair stays connected to butt during parade.

As I walked to my apartment, I was worried that I was going to forget all my mental notes before I could put them into action. You know me. I have a thought and it's with me for five or ten minutes. Then, all of a sudden, it packs its bags and takes off for a journey into the unknown. Sometimes it returns, and sometimes it just shoots off into the universe and never comes back even for a visit. I'm not like Frankie, who remembers every thought he ever had.

I opened our apartment door with my key—which took about five minutes to find. During the time I was downstairs in the clubhouse, my key must have moved from pocket to pocket, just to throw me off. I could have sworn I'd put it in my shirt pocket, but I found it in the back pocket of my jeans, buried in between some old gummy bears. I had to peel those sticky suckers off the key before I could fit it into the lock.

By the time I finally got into our apartment, I was so ready to start my costume that I felt like I was going to pop. I must have been really distracted because I almost tripped over our dachshund, Cheerio. He was waiting for me in the front hall, doing what he likes to do best—spinning around in circles.

"Slow down, boy," I said, trying to scratch him behind the ears, which was hard to do since he was spinning so fast. "If you keep going like that, you're going to lift off like a helicopter."

Cheerio collapsed in a dizzy heap like he always does, and I took off down the entry hall. Unfortunately, as I hit the living room, I ran smack into my dad.

"Hey, Dad. I have the greatest idea for a costume in the entire history of Halloween!" I said to him.

"Not so fast, mister," he said. "Halloween comes after . . ."

"Tonight," I said. "You don't have to tell me that Halloween is tomorrow, Dad. I'm counting the hours until the school parade."

"If you'd let me finish my sentence, Hank, I was about to say that Halloween comes after homework."

"You're kidding me, right, Dad?"

"Do I look like I'm kidding?"

I looked at his face. His glasses were sitting on top of his forehead where he usually wears them when he's working a crossword puzzle. His teeth weren't showing, like they do when he smiles. His eyes weren't squinty, like they are when something amuses him. His mouth wasn't turned up at the edges, like it does when he's laughing. Nope, I saw not one bit of kidding in his face. Not even a teensy, tiny bit.

"Dad, you're not going to make me do homework on the night before Halloween, are you?"

I pleaded. "I've got to make my costume."

"Halloween comes second. First comes math, reading, social studies."

"Actually, that would make Halloween come fourth," my sister, Emily, piped up from the dining room, "after math, reading, and . . ."

"We can all remember what Dad said, Emily," I snapped. The last thing I needed now was Miss Perfect ticking off all the subjects I had homework in.

I walked into the dining room, hoping my dad wouldn't follow me. No luck. He did.

"Do you have homework in every subject?" he asked. Boy, his curiosity about my homework was out of control.

I looked around the dining room, trying to come up with a decent argument about why tonight was not the night to get serious about homework. I was desperate. Emily and her nerd boyfriend, Robert Upchurch, were sitting at the dining-room table, working on their Halloween costumes. They had decided to go as twin flu germs, which will give you an idea of how much fun they are.

Emily was using Play-Doh to make pus

pockets, and Robert had yellow and green markers to color in infected areas. And get this, they had figured out that their costumes would double as a science project. That way, if they didn't win top prize in the Halloween parade, at least they'd get extra credit for educating the students at PS 87 about runny noses. And, by the way, they don't need extra credit because they're each getting an A-plus in science. Or even higher.

What's higher than an A-plus? Maybe an A-plus-plus. I wouldn't know because I've never gotten one. I've only traveled to C-ville and parts south.

"Emily's making her costume," I said to my dad. "I don't see her doing homework."

"That's because it's already done, doofus," Emily answered. "As a matter of fact, I did it the minute I walked in the house. Didn't I, Robert?"

"Indeedy do, you did," Robert said.

Then he laughed his snorty little hippo laugh, like he had said something funny. Robert is so skinny that when he laughs, you can see his ribs moving around in his chest. I saw him laugh once during a swim class at the 98th Street YMCA when he didn't have a shirt on, and you could have mistaken him for a skeleton in the Museum of Natural History. Fortunately, he keeps his chest covered most of the time with the white shirt and tie that he wears every day to school. You heard me. I said a tie!

"Some of us know the importance of time management," Emily said. "That's why I like to complete my homework as early in the day as possible."

My sister. She can have a real attitude when she wants to.

"For your information, time management and I happen to be very good friends," I shot back at her. "I can manage my time any time I want to."

"Oh really? Is that why just today we got another note from Ms. Adolf saying you were missing homework assignments?"

Emily, Emily, Emily! Why do you have a mouth if all you're going to use it for is to rat me out to Mom and Dad?

I was hoping no one had noticed that note. I had left it on the table in the entry hall but slid most of it under the flower vase my mom keeps there.

Thanks, Emily, for pointing it out to everyone. Miss Rat Mouth strikes again!

"At least I don't choose to spend my time making pus pockets," I answered. I had to get tough with her if she was going to bring up Ms. Adolf in front of my dad. "And speaking of pus pockets—Robert, it's always good to see you."

I turned, stomped off into my room, and slammed the door.

About one-third of a second later, the door to my room blasted open. I think you can probably guess who was standing there.

"Hi, Dad," I said, without looking up.

"We're not finished, Hank," he said.

"I know. I know. Homework first. Costume later."

"You'll thank me for this one day," my dad said.

I've learned something in my almost eleven years as Hank Zipzer. When a grown-up tells you that you'll thank them one day for *this*, it means you are about to have to do something you really, really hate. I pulled my math workbook from my backpack and wondered when the day would actually come that I'd be thanking my dad for making me do long division. When I was ninety-two? Or sixty-six?

One thing I knew for sure, it wasn't going to be tonight.

CHAPTER 3

I DID MY HOMEWORK in record time. I'm not going to say much more about it, because we all know that doing homework was invented by King Boring of Boringville, which is found just on the outskirts of I-Can't-Find-the-Answers-in-My-Brainville. I'll bet you've visited there yourself.

But since I know you're probably curious, though, I'll give you a few of my tips on how I manage to finish homework in record time.

HANK ZIPZER'S TOP-TEN TIPS FOR GETTING YOUR HOMEWORK DONE REALLY, REALLY FAST

1. If it's math homework, skip the odd problems and only do the even ones. Tell your teacher that you're allergic to odd

problems and when you do them your scalp itches like crazy.

2. If they're short-answer questions, take the directions seriously and give short answers. As in *one* word.

3. If they're multiple-choice questions, don't stress yourself out worrying about which answer is right. Take your best shot and move on.

4. If you have to write a paragraph, remember that there's no law that says it has to make sense.

5. If you have to write an essay, well, sorry, but there's no quick way around that. Once, I told Ms. Adolf that I couldn't write the essay because I had so many ideas for it, I couldn't decide which one to write. (She didn't buy it, but, hey, that doesn't mean it won't work for you.)

6. About extra credit problems . . . leave those to the brainiacs like Heather Payne. You don't know her yet, but you'll read all about her in Chapter 16.

7. See number 10.

8. See number 10.

9. See number 10.
10. There's nothing wrong with skipping a few questions. See numbers 7 to 9 as examples.

CHAPTER 4

I am a
Tonsil

With the help of Hank's Top-Ten Tips, I finished my homework and got to the good stuff—my costume. My mom was a champ and helped me cut up her red-and-white checkered tablecloth. While we were cutting the tabletop out of cardboard, she made one of her famous Randi Zipzer suggestions.

"Hank, sweetie," she said, eyeing the glass of breadsticks I was planning to put on the tabletop. "Those white-flour breadsticks are so not body friendly. Let me give you some whole grain, flaxseed-infused, toasted crisps instead."

My mom never gives up trying to change the world, one healthy food at a time. She believes in health food like I believe in the Mets. All the way. Do or die. Till the very end. Like last week in our deli, the Crunchy Pickle, she introduced liverwurst made from broccoli instead of liver.

Personally, I wouldn't eat liverwurst no matter what it's made from. But let me warn you—if you ever find yourself inside the door of the Crunchy Pickle, I suggest you run as fast as you can away from the brocci-wurst. The smell of it has been known to separate a human nose from its face. In fact, the alley in back of our deli is filled with separated noses bouncing around on their tips.

That night, I was completely involved in making my costume. I didn't even take a five-minute break for cereal and milk, one of my favorite nighttime snacks.

And my mom got really involved in making a costume for Cheerio. Emily and Robert had decided that they wanted him to be a tonsil so they could surround him in their flu-germ costumes. They thought that if he growled at them, it would show how tonsils do battle with flu germs. After I pointed out that no kid in his or her right mind even knows what a tonsil looks like, my mom made a little hat for Cheerio out of cardboard that said "I Am a Tonsil." When she tried to put it on him, Cheerio ran away and hid under my bed. He's a smart dog, Cheerio is.

He's not going to be anyone's tonsil.

When I finally finished my costume, it was way past my bedtime. My dad, who doubles as the Bedtime Police in our house, had fallen asleep in his chair doing a crossword puzzle. He was probably dreaming of a four-letter word for a web-footed bird related to the goose family.

I'm tempted to describe to you every detail of how I made my costume. But instead, I'm going to let you be surprised at what it looked like.

Sorry, guys. You're just going to have to read the next chapter.

CHAPTER 5

WHEN I WALKED INTO SCHOOL the next morning, I could feel the buzz in the halls. Everyone was excited about the Halloween parade. It was scheduled for lunch period, to give us all time to eat quickly and change into our Halloween costumes. Then at exactly twelve twenty-five, we were all to line up in the school yard and march around in a circle. The little kids' parents were invited to come and watch, and a lot of the neighborhood people looked in through the chain-link fence. It was a chance to strut around in your costume and feel proud of being a student at PS 87.

Everyone in my class was talking before the bell rang.

"I got the grossest costume," Nick McKelty bragged, as usual.

"Mine is grosser," said Luke Whitman, the

king of gross. I'd bet on Luke.

"We're twin princesses," said Katie Sperling and Kim Paulson.

"That is so lame," McKelty said, laughing at them.

That McKelty, he really knows how to charm the girls.

We could hardly stop talking, even when Ms. Adolf called the class to order.

The fun-loving Ms. Adolf came to school in a witch's costume—which, by the way, turned out not to be a costume. It was her everyday outfit. She looks more like a witch than anyone you've ever met. I think she is really a witch. At least the part of her that hands out grades and homework. I know that for sure.

Ms. Adolf did try to get into the Halloween spirit a little bit. Don't get me wrong. She didn't really throw herself into it like Mr. Sicilian, the fourth-grade teacher, who dressed up like a hockey player and skated into class on Rollerblades. Nothing that cool for old Ms. Adolf. After the bell rang, she went to her top drawer and took out a big, warty rubber nose that looked like a tree branch. She strapped it to her face just before she rapped on her desk with a ruler and made her festive Halloween announcement.

"Pupils," she began, sounding like a person whose nose was covered in green rubber, "in honor of the Halloween parade, I have designed a special morning activity."

Wow. For a tiny moment, I had hope that there was going to be candy in our fifth-grade class. I closed my eyes and saw bags of Skittles and Kit Kats and Baby Ruths and sour apple gummy bears. My mouth started to water before I could stop it.

"This morning, we will enjoy a Halloween spelling adventure," Ms. Adolf went on. "The words on our spelling quiz will all be related to the holiday—such as *ghostly*, *broomstick*, *vampire*, and, yes, *cauldron*."

My mouth dried up as quickly as you can say *cauldron*. Visions of green gummy bears were replaced by visions of red pencil marks all over my spelling test—with a big red 39 percent at the top of the page.

Oh, Ms. Adolf, were you born without a fun gene, or is this something you work at?

My hand shot up into the air.

"Ms. Adolf, when will we be able to change into our costumes for the Halloween parade?" I asked.

"Henry, how can you think of a parade when you have the opportunity to participate in a spellfest?" she asked, burning her batlike eyes into my forehead.

"It's easy, Ms. Adolf," I answered. "Because one is fun and the other is torture. *Torture*—a Halloween word, by the way."

The class started to laugh—even Heather Payne, who doesn't laugh out loud until Ms. Adolf laughs first, which is never.

"Zipperbutt's just mad because he can't spell!" shouted Nick McKelty.

"I can spell the word *jerk*," I said to McKelty.

"Oh yeah? Let's hear it," he said, sticking his huge beefy face in front of mine.

"N-I-C-K," I said.

Everyone in the class laughed and clapped at the same time. The one thing you can say about Nick McKelty is that he's not the most popular guy in the fifth grade. I guess nobody likes a bully. In fact, his only real friend is his girl-friend, Joelle Atkins, who mostly talks to him on her cell phone so she doesn't have to look at his squiggly teeth all filled with cookie crumbs and wadded-up string cheese.

Ms. Adolf doesn't like it when we laugh in class. She clapped her hands together, stomped one of her gray shoes that she wears to go with her all-gray witch clothes, and shouted, "Pupils, control yourselves!"

When we didn't stop laughing right away, she got a big red blotch on her neck. That happens when she gets angry. I stared at it. I thought this one was shaped like a pumpkin, but maybe I was just in a Halloween mood.

"Henry," Ms. Adolf said, "are you looking for a visit with Principal Love?"

"He is a very nice human being, and I always enjoy visiting his office, but if it's okay with you, I think I'll pass on the invitation," I said. "Thanks, anyway."

Now the class really howled.

"Zip, she's going to destroy you," Frankie whispered from his desk across the aisle. "Knock it off."

It's a funny thing about when I make the class laugh. It makes me feel good, because I'm giving the kids a chuckle and, believe me, there aren't that many chuckles in a day spent with Ms. Adolf. On the other hand, I know that those chuckles will lead me directly into detention or the principal's office or worse yet: extra homework.

"Henry, tonight you're going to write a paragraph on the usefulness of raising your hand before speaking," Ms. Adolf said. "Have it on my desk first thing tomorrow morning."

Am I a mind reader, or what?

"But, Ms. Adolf, tonight is Halloween," I protested. "And there is candy in every apartment of our building, just waiting for me to get it and eat it!"

"Sugar makes the brain soggy," she said.

Frankie shot me the look that said "Shut Up Now." I took his advice. I was about to answer her but stopped myself.

Ms. Adolf walked up and down the aisles, handing a piece of paper to each of us. The thought of a spelling quiz settled me down right away. For me, nothing takes the fun out of a day like a spelling quiz.

"Pencils up. Eyes on your own paper," Ms. Adolf said. And the fun-filled Halloween spelling quiz was underway.

It seemed like forever until lunch, but it finally came. After we ate, we were allowed to go to the bathroom to change into our costumes.

I hurried ahead of Frankie so I could grab the first stall and lock the door. I didn't want anyone to see my costume before it was completely ready. I don't know much about parades, but I know that you've got to make a big entrance if you want to grab the spotlight. I was prepared for that.

From inside the stall, I could hear the other boys getting ready. They were talking in really excited voices.

"Can you pass me that bottle of fake blood?" Ryan Shimozato said.

"That scar is disgusto. Very cool," his buddy Hector said.

"Hey, what'd you use for those guts?" Luke Whitman wanted to know.

How typical. You think Halloween, and

you go right to the usual—blood, guts, gore, eyeballs, mummies.

Not you, Hank. You are a creative thinker.

As I swung the tablecloth over my head and loaded the breadsticks into the glass in my hand, I felt really good.

Hank Zipzer, you've done it again. Original has got to be your middle name.

CHAPTER 6

WHOOPS.

I'd like to apply to officially change my middle name from Original to WHAT WAS I THINKING?????

CHAPTER 7

IT STARTED WHEN I made my entrance. Everyone else was already lined up in the school yard. I came down the stairs alone, feeling great.

But the one thing I hadn't taken into account when I built my costume was the size of the door to the yard in relation to the size of my tabletop. Let me just sum it up this way. The door was smaller than I would have hoped for. Much smaller. The fact is, I couldn't fit through it.

I tried it frontways. No go. I tried it sideways. No go. Finally, I had to slant the tabletop practically straight up and down so I could fit through the door. I turned sideways, held my breath, and squeezed through. But even then, I slammed into the door on the way out and knocked off the left part of the tabletop. Or maybe it was the right part. I can never tell.

And in this stressful situation, it was impossible. Anyway, whichever side it was, it was hanging down like a bird with a broken wing.

"Hi, Hank," said Mason, who was dressed up as a pirate. He's my little pal from kindergarten. "Is that a cape you're wearing?"

"I'm a little busy right now, matey," I said. "Can we talk later?"

"Sure," he said. "I like your cape. But it smells weird."

At first, I couldn't figure out what he meant. Then it hit me. The smell, I mean. As I was trying to squeeze through the door, I had knocked over the bottle of garlic-scented olive oil that was taped onto the tabletop. The olive oil had spilled all over the place. I could now feel it seeping into my T-shirt and running down my arm.

You know how they say garlic is supposed to keep vampires away? Well, let me tell you, it also works on second-, third-, fourth-, and fifth-graders. As I walked to the yard, everyone backed away.

And about the breadsticks. Just as I joined the line of kids in the parade, I bent down to scratch my ankle, and the breadsticks slipped right out of the plastic glass that was taped to the other side of the table.

Crunch! I stepped on them, at which point they were transformed from breadsticks into bread crumbs. I tried to scrape them up from the asphalt and put them back in the glass. I couldn't get most of them, but the few I did get looked like ground-up grayish crumbs at the bottom of the glass. Even I have to admit, they lost a little of their Italian appeal.

"Check out Zipperbutt!" Nick McKelty was the first to yell. "What are you supposed to be, creep?"

McKelty was decked out in gruesome, top to bottom. He had a bleeding eye pasted to his forehead. He had a bleeding scar pasted to his cheek. He had bleeding bandages wrapped around his arm. He had bleeding knees, bleeding elbows, bleeding toes, bleeding guts. He was, as I had always thought of him, an open, disgusting sore.

"Unlike yourself," I said, "I have used my creativity to come up with an original, if smelly, costume."

"You stink like a garbage Dumpster," he said.

"For your information, I am a dining table in a great Italian restaurant."

"What's that got to do with Halloween?" the Great Brain asked.

"I think Hank had a very clever idea," Ashley spoke up. She was dressed in a dolphin costume, which she had covered with turquoise, gray, and white rhinestones. She waved one of her fins at me and whispered, "If you walk around a little, the air might tone down some of the smell."

"An Italian restaurant!" McKelty shouted. I guess the idea had finally seeped through his thick skull into his brain. "That is so lame. Only a kindergartner would think that's funny."

"I'm a kindergartner," Mason said. "And I don't think it's funny."

"See that! Not even a dumb five-year-old thinks it's funny," McKelty hooted.

"You're very mean," Mason said to McKelty, and ran back to where the kindergartners were gathered.

"Good riddance," McKelty hollered after him. Then he turned back to me. "Check me out, Zipperhead. My Halloween costume is cool. Blood and guts. That's where it's at."

"I think Nick's costume is the greatest," Joelle Atkins chimed in. You have to think everything Nick does is the greatest if you want to be his girlfriend, which I can't imagine anyone but Joelle ever wanting to be.

"Of course you do," I said to her. "He's bleeding everywhere and you're dressed as a Band-Aid."

"I am not a Band-Aid," she said. "I am a cell phone. Can't you see the numbers written on my back?"

Joelle is totally in love with her cell phone. She walks around with it strapped to her wrist at all times, which is weird, because no one ever calls her. I guess she's hoping someone will. It didn't surprise me that her costume was a cell phone. She turned around and sure enough, there was a cell-phone number pad constructed on her back.

"I bet if you dialed her number, there'd be nobody home," Frankie whispered to me.

I didn't even have time to laugh, because just then I heard Emily calling me from across in the school yard. I looked around and saw her on the handball court where the fourth-graders were lining up. She and Robert were leading the pack in their flu-germ costumes. They both waved at me, looking really proud of themselves. Geeky as they were, you have to give them credit for bravery and originality. There wasn't another flu germ on the playground, except maybe the real ones living in Luke Whitman's nose.

Suddenly, Emily and Robert bolted out of line and ran up to the little stage that had been set up with a microphone for Principal Love.

"Hi, everyone," Emily yelled into the microphone. "We're flu germs."

"Don't come too close," Robert added, "or you'll catch us! Get it? Catch us!"

Then he snorted his geeky hippo laugh into the microphone. The microphone made it sound way geekier than it is in real life, if that's possible.

"You two are disgusting!" McKelty shouted out. "You make me sick. Get it? Flu germs make me sick!"

A bunch of kids laughed. Emily looked really hurt, and poor Robert just looked confused. I felt red-hot anger rise up from the bottom of my tablecloth all the way past my butt chair and into my head. Who did that McKelty think he was? I mean, it's one thing if he wanted to embarrass me in front of everyone. But only a total bully would pick on Emily and Robert.

I spun around and started over to him. I wasn't going to let him get away with that. But I was stopped dead in my tracks by Frankie.

"Ow!" he said. "Watch it, Zip."

My tabletop had butted him right in the head and gotten caught in the face mask of his football helmet. He was going as Tiki Barber, his favorite player on the New York Giants. But in the war between my tabletop and his football helmet, the helmet won. As he disconnected his face mask from the cardboard, a chunk of my table collapsed under me. I watched helplessly as the plastic bottle with the candle slid down the tabletop and onto the playground. Ryan Shimozato came running by and stepped on it. I heard it crunch beneath his foot.

"Sorry, dude," he said. "I didn't mean to break your . . . uh . . . whatever this is."

At that moment, Principal Love stepped up to the microphone.

"Attention, students. I now declare the PS

87 Halloween Day Parade officially open. As I always say, a parade is an occasion for parading."

Principal Love likes to say everything twice. I looked down at the smashed bottle and waited.

"So join me now," he went on, "as I lead you into the world of celebratory spirits and marauding goblins. Yes, a parade is an occasion for parading."

Bingo! There it was.

He waved his banner, which was black with orange pumpkins on it. Then he leaned into the microphone and let out what he thought was a scary laugh. It turns out it was actually very scary, because it caused so much screeching feedback over the loudspeaker that a bunch of the kindergartners started to cry.

Principal Love wasn't even aware that he had frightened the little kids half to death. He just set off marching around the playground, waving the banner. A lot of kids lined up to follow him. Pretty soon, we were all marching in a circle, with the teachers and the parents of the little kids surrounding us and applauding as we marched.

I had to pull myself together to try to march with confidence. True, I had gotten off to a bad start. The garlic-scented olive oil had spilled, the breadsticks had turned to dust, the candlestick was crunched, and my tabletop was definitely drooping. But I reminded myself that I was the only Italian table in the parade. So I put my shoulders back, held my chin up, and took off with confidence . . . until . . .

. . . I marched past the kindergarten teachers, Mr. Zilke and Ms. Warner.

"I wonder who's eating garlic bread?" Mr. Zilke said.

"Boy, that's a strong smell," Ms. Warner agreed. "Smells like someone took a bath in garlic cloves."

As I walked by, I saw them both hold their noses. That didn't help my confidence any. Call me crazy, but I don't like to think I stink so bad that people have to hold their noses around me.

I noticed that many of the neighbors who were looking through the chain-link fence were pointing at me and laughing. And not necessarily in a good way.

Why hadn't I listened to Frankie and Ashley?

They had tried to warn me that this wouldn't work out. Sometimes I really hate my brain for not being able to listen when smart people are giving me good advice.

Here's a tip for you to remember next time you're in a parade: You shouldn't be thinking about other things while you're marching, especially when you're wearing a large, almost square tabletop.

Boom!

I hadn't noticed that the line had stopped while I kept marching. The *boom* I'm referring to was me crashing into Principal Love's balding head.

"Oww!" he screamed as he dropped the school banner and fell face-first into the punch bowl that was waiting for everybody at the end of the parade. Without going into detail, let me just say that when he came up for air, he was shouting my name.

"Mr. Zipzer!" he gargled. "Your costume is a menace!"

"It's stupid, too!" McKelty yelled.

"And smelly," Joelle added.

"But it was a great idea," I said.

43

"Do us all a favor, Zipzer," McKelty said. "Next time you get a bright idea, just remember, it's probably really stupid like everything else you do."

For once, I had to admit that maybe McKelty was right.

Halloween was all about gushing blood and gory guts.

And me? Well, I was all about stinky olive oil and broken breadsticks.

I looked over at McKelty, who was still laughing at me. And all I wanted was to disappear.

CHAPTER 8

NINE HALLOWEEN THINGS
I SHOULD HAVE GONE AS

1. A nine-foot-tall emperor penguin that looks friendly but when it wraps its wings around McKelty it would squeeze him like the slimy fish that he is.

2. The ghoul from Zeon whose claws shoot out slime that would harden around McKelty and glue him to the playground where the kindergartners would use him as a jungle gym.

3. A giant eyeball that squirts out eyeball gel, and when it lands on McKelty removes every hair from his head. Everyone would call him Eyeball Head for the rest of his life. (Come to think of it, that name is probably too nice for him.)

45

4. A walking hand that is trained to pinch McKelty in the butt twenty-four/seven.

5. A crazed bowling ball that would follow McKelty around and knock him down every three-and-a-half minutes. It would give new meaning to the word "strike."

6. A zombie that lives in McKelty's closet and howls every time he opens it up. Wait a minute. The smell of McKelty's old gym socks would probably drive that zombie out of there and back to Zombieland forever.

7. Ms. Adolf in her all-gray outfit, who constantly gives McKelty a spelling test of really long words he's never heard of before, like *cornucopia* or *epiphany*.

8. I could keep going forever, but then I'd never get to tell you what happened next, so I'll stop now. Okay, maybe just one more, because these feel so good I don't really want to stop.

9. A human vacuum cleaner that would suck McKelty up and put him in a bag filled with carpet dust and iguana droppings. (Oh, Hank Zipzer, you are on fire! It's moments like these when I really love my brain.)

CHAPTER 9

IN CASE YOU COULDN'T TELL from that list, I was boiling mad at Nick McKelty. He had no right to make fun of my costume. He had no right to make fun of my sister. He had no right to make fun of me. And most of all, he had no right to call me stupid in front of the whole school and neighborhood.

And I told all that to my grandpa, Papa Pete, as he walked me home from school that day. I'm really lucky to have a grandpa who understands when I'm mad and lets me spew it all out and doesn't tell me to watch my language and not use angry words.

"Who is he to make me feel like a jerk in front of everyone in the whole school?" I said to Papa Pete as we headed to Harvey's, our favorite pizza stop at the corner of Broadway and 78th. "He's just a big bully who thinks it's cool to make fun of everyone else."

"That's what bullies do," Papa Pete said. "They attack first. And think later."

"Not in McKelty's case," I said. "He never thinks at all."

We crossed the street and walked by the West Side Bagel Shop and Wonder Nails Salon, which meant that we were only a couple of doors away from Harvey's. I could feel my nose being attacked by the delicious smell of pizza pie, my favorite smell in the whole wide world.

"Papa Pete, I would never think of making someone else feel so bad all the time."

"That's because you have a good heart," Papa Pete said. "And you care about other people's feelings. Maybe your learning challenges have helped with that."

I stopped dead in my tracks, right in front of the glass door to Harvey's. No one, and I mean no one, had ever even hinted that my learning challenges could be good for anything except frustrating me.

"How would my learning challenges help me with anything?"

"Well, Hankie," Papa Pete said, smiling at me

from below his furry mustache, "you are very well aware of how difficult things can be, and because you know that about yourself, it makes you sensitive to how other people are feeling. That's a lesson you can't learn in a book."

Papa Pete gave my shoulder a big squeeze with one hand, then opened the door to Harvey's with the other one.

I thought about what he'd said as I slid onto a stool and breathed in the wonderful smell of Parmesan, tomato, and pepperoni all sizzling in the oven. Papa Pete did have a point. Not to brag, but a lot of people tell me I'm a pretty nice guy. Frankie and Ashley always say that I'm a good friend. And my mom says that I have a kind streak as wide as the whole Atlantic Ocean.

Wow. Maybe if I had been born with a perfect brain, I'd be cranky like Ms. Adolf. Or mean like Nick McKelty.

I made a mental note to think about that more sometime when my stomach wasn't screaming out for pizza.

I did a three-sixty spin on the shiny silver stool—it's part of my Harvey's tradition before ordering my usual: a slice of pizza with mushrooms and extra cheese. But before I could even order, Harvey came up and brought me a really gooey slice loaded with mushrooms and extra cheese. The great thing about having a neighborhood pizza place is that they know what you want before you even say it.

"Thanks, Harvey," I said.

"I'll be right back with your Sprite," he said to me. "And your coffee," he said to Papa Pete, who had already helped himself to a crumb donut they keep on a cake plate on the counter.

I took a bite of my pizza, but before I could even swallow it, I had an idea that was so powerful I had to blurt it out loud with my mouth full, even though this is not allowed in the Zipzer family.

"I really want to scare Nick McKelty out of his socks," I said, spitting a few crust crumbs out into the air in front of me.

"Getting even, are you?" Papa Pete said.

"I just want to prove to that guy that I'm not the wimp he thinks I am."

"Don't you know that on your own?"

"The only thing I know is that the guy made fun of me and of Emily, too. And the other kids laughed, so they must've agreed with him."

"Not necessarily. Maybe they just thought he was funny."

"Listen, Papa Pete," I said, pulling a long string of cheese off my lower lip and popping it into my mouth. "McKelty thinks I'm a wimp, and I think I acted like one. That makes me feel bad."

Papa Pete took a sip of his coffee. He looked at me and nodded. Then he put his hand on my head and tousled my hair like he used to do when I was little. He doesn't do that so much now that I put gel in my hair.

"Feeling bad is not good," he said. "Feeling good is good. Eating pizza is good. Bowling three strikes in a row is good. Having a fun Halloween is good."

"So far, this Halloween hasn't been much fun," I told Papa Pete.

Papa Pete took a big bite of his crumb donut. He can polish off a donut in two bites. He chewed for a moment, took another sip of coffee to wash it down, and then turned to me.

"Why don't you build a haunted house?" he suggested. "The best Halloween I can remember was when your mother and her sister, your aunt Maxine, built a haunted house in the garage. The neighborhood kids came from blocks around to see it."

Papa Pete described how they put wet grapes in a bowl and told the kids they were eyeballs. I thought to myself, *Hank, you could do that.*

He told me how they boiled spaghetti until it was mush and told the kids it was ghoul brains. I thought to myself, *Hank, you could do that.*

When he described how they had their dog, Annie, howl into a tape recorder until she sounded like a ghost living in the subway tunnels of New York, I thought to myself, *Hank, Cheerio could do that.*

My mind raced as my mouth chewed.

Sure, we didn't have a garage to use for a haunted house. But we had a living room and sheets we could use to make walls. And I could turn out all the living-room lights to make it dark and creepy. Wait! My parents even had that black light they used for a sixties party once that makes everything white glow in the dark.

This was it! This was how I could turn the most awful Halloween ever into the most amazing Halloween of my life.

All I had to do was put together the scariest, creepiest haunted house ever. Sure, it would be fun to invite a bunch of kids from my class. But I have to confess, I was thinking of fun second. I was thinking of revenge first!

Wouldn't it be great to invite one very special guest and scare him out of his mind?

You guessed it.

Nick "The Tick" McKelty.

Hey, Nick. BOO!!!!!!!!!!!!!!!!!!!

CHAPTER 10

I MADE PAPA PETE RUN all the way home from Harvey's with me, which is fine with him because he's in great shape for a guy who's sixty-nine years old. He is a champion Ping-Pong player, not to mention the best bowler on the Chopped Livers, his league team at McKelty's Roll 'N Bowl. He even holds the all-time strike record for one night when he bowled four strikes in a row.

"I'm going to need help building the haunted house," I told Papa Pete as we pushed open the door to my apartment.

"You don't have much time," Papa Pete said, checking his watch. "It's almost four o'clock."

"I'll put a sign on the front door that the haunted house opens at seven o'clock. That gives us four hours to put it together."

"Hankie, slow down for a minute and

concentrate," Papa Pete said. He held out his arm, pushed up the sleeve of his red running jacket, and pointed to his wristwatch.

"Look at my watch. Here's the four, and there's the seven," he said, pointing to the numbers. "Now tell me again. How many hours do you have to finish the haunted house?"

I had to concentrate on slowing my brain down to look at the numbers on his watch. Seven take away four is . . .

"Three," I answered. "Right. We have three hours to finish. Thanks, Papa Pete. You know me and numbers. We're not exactly best friends."

Papa Pete just smiled. He never makes me feel bad when I get things wrong. That's one thing I love about him.

Cheerio came running out of the bedroom to say hello to us. I could tell he had been asleep because he was still yawning as he trotted out.

"Great news, boy," I said, scratching him behind the ears. "We're going to build a haunted house."

He flopped down in front of me and rolled over on his back to get his tummy scratched. He felt all warm, like he always does when he's been asleep.

"That may not be such great news for Cheerio," Papa Pete said. "Dogs don't really understand about Halloween. The haunted house could scare him."

"Not my Cheerio," I said, giving him the special Double-Trouble-Tummy-Ear Scratch I had invented just for him. "He's no scaredy-cat. Are you, boy?"

Cheerio wagged his tail and seemed really happy. I was sorry that I had to cut our scratch-fest short, but time was ticking by and I had a lot to do.

"So three hours," I said, jumping to my feet and pulling off my jacket. "That's enough time, isn't it, Papa Pete? It's got to be. That's all I got."

"Maybe you could use a little help from your friends," Papa Pete said. He sat down at the green desk in the living room and looked for some paper in the drawer.

"Once again, great idea, Papa Pete," I said. "I'll call Ashley and Frankie immediately. Well, not exactly immediately, because I have another call to make immediately."

I ran to the phone in the kitchen and pulled out the directory from my school, which my mom leaves on the yellow-tile counter under the phone. I looked up Nick McKelty's name under the N's. It wasn't there.

Why wouldn't it be there? I was pretty sure I was spelling his name right. N-I-C-K.

I tried N-O-C-K and then N-E-C-K, but I still couldn't find a listing. I was just starting to get really frustrated when I got a brainstorm.

I bet it's alphabetized under his last name.

It's just like grown-ups to do a crazy thing like that! I flipped through the pages of the directory really fast until I got to the M's. I looked down the list until I came to it. There it was. McKelty, Nick.

Way to go, Hankster. You've got to think like a grown-up. Put yourself in their place. Put last names first and first names last.

I could hardly wait to dial that number. I purposely tried to slow my brain down as I read the number. Lots of times, I flip numbers around when I read them. It's like I don't see them in the right order.

Concentrate on the numbers, Hank. Get

them right. You don't want to wind up calling the Central Park Zoo.

Actually, I could probably reach McKelty there, too. In the ape cage.

I dialed carefully, and while the phone was ringing, I grabbed a dish towel and put it over the receiver. I had seen this trick in an old movie once that I watched with my dad when I was home with a sore throat. A detective in a weird plaid hat was calling his cousin who was planning to rob a bank. The detective didn't want his voice to be recognized, so he put a towel over the receiver. His own cousin never even knew it was him. I didn't know if the dish towel would work, but I figured if it worked for the guy in the weird plaid hat, it was worth a shot.

"Hello," said Nick the Tick on the other end of the phone.

You dialed it right, Hank. Now go for it. Lay it on.

I lowered my voice as low as it would go.

"Nick McKelty," I growled into the dish towel, "are you man enough to risk being scared all the way to Pluto and beyond?"

Wow, where did that sentence come from? It was great!

"Who is this?" McKelty said.

"No questions," I growled into the phone. "Just listen. Tonight at seven-thirty sharp, and I mean like a razor, you are to come meet the ghoul of all ghouls, the terror of all terrors, the zomb of all zombies . . ."

"Hey, who *is* this?" I couldn't tell if McKelty sounded annoyed or scared.

"Are you a scaredy-cat?" I went on, having fun with my own voice. "Is your blood running cold? Are your nervous zones sweating yet? Or will you show up?"

"Show up where?" McKelty asked. I had him! He was buying it!

"210 West 78th Street," I said. "Apartment 10A. The home of your deepest fears."

"Hey, I know that address. Is that you, Zipperbutt?"

"I live in Hank Zipzer's house," I growled. "But I am not him. I am the ghost of Halloween past, the restless spirit, come to haunt the living and terrify the weak."

"You don't scare me," McKelty said, even

though his voice sounded somewhat higher than usual.

"Then come and test your nerves," I said. "We'll find out if you are the man you say you are."

"I'll be there," McKelty said. "I'm not afraid of you."

I hung up.

"Yes," I said, pumping my fists in the air.

I can honestly say that was the best phone call I have ever made. Even better than when I called my sister and told her I was an iguana psychiatrist and that her pet iguana, Katherine, was having a nervous breakdown and needed to be institutionalized. She let out a scream so loud, I almost went deaf. Man, that was fun.

Back to the plan, Hank. Don't let your mind wander.

I picked up the phone and dialed Frankie.

"Can you meet me in the lobby in five minutes? And pick up Ashley. We have important stuff to do."

"Talk to me, Zip. What important stuff?"

"You're not going to believe the plan I just came up with. Trust me."

Before Frankie could answer, I hung up the phone and ran back into the living room where Papa Pete was still sitting at the green desk, writing. It looked like he was working on some kind of a list.

"Papa Pete, you can't be writing now. We have haunted house stuff to do."

"First of all, Hankie, I left a note for your father, telling him about the haunted house. He'll read it when he brings Emily home from her Girl Scout meeting."

"Great thinking yet again, Papa Pete," I said. It hadn't occurred to me that it was a good idea to let your parents know when you're turning their living room into the scariest place on earth.

"And second of all, I made you a list of all the instructions for the haunted house. Right here is everything you need to know."

He held up a piece of paper covered with writing. Wow, that was a lot of words.

"Why are you making a list?" I asked him. "Aren't you going to be here to help us?"

"I can't," Papa Pete said. "I have a date with the rear end of an elephant costume."

I just stood there for a minute, letting the words sink in to my head. I think they went in for maybe a second or two, but then my brain just spit them back out again.

"Papa Pete, that is the weirdest sentence I've ever heard you say," was all I could answer.

"That's because it's the weirdest date I've ever had," Papa Pete said with a smile. "Mrs. Fink and I are going to the Halloween costume party at McKelty's Roll 'N Bowl."

Our next-door neighbor Mrs. Fink has had a crush on Papa Pete for a long time. At least, I think it's a crush. I'm not sure what you call it when older people like each other in a romantic way. But let me be clear about this. The crush is definitely one-way. Mrs. Fink's crush on Papa Pete is way bigger than his crush on her. At least, that's what I had always thought.

"You asked Mrs. Fink out on a date?" I couldn't believe my ears!

"She was the only person I know large enough to fill out the hind end of the elephant costume I rented," Papa Pete explained.

He had a point. There was a whole lot of Mrs. Fink. She must have been enjoying her own cherry strudel for many years, which I can understand because, as I've mentioned, her strudel could be the best in the world.

"But, Papa Pete, we need you," I said.

"The Chopped Livers need me, too," he answered. "Our team has challenged the Lucky Strikers in the costume contest. My teammates are counting on me."

"But I don't know if I can do this without you," I said.

The haunted house was a lot to take on by ourselves with no grown-ups to help. My mom wasn't coming back from the deli until almost seven. And even though my dad would be back from Emily's Girl Scout party pretty soon, he wouldn't be much help. Scary fun isn't exactly his specialty, unless it's a clue in a crossword puzzle.

"You'll do fine," Papa Pete said. "I've written out all the instructions for you."

Papa Pete handed me a piece of lined notebook paper that was filled with writing. I looked at it quickly, and the letters started to dance all over the page. That happens to me all the time, especially with anything written on narrow-lined paper. Words never stay where they're supposed to be. They jump from line to line and zoom all over the page. Some of them even dive right off the edge and I miss them completely. My eyes get really tired trying to follow them.

I didn't have time for dancing letters right then, so I took Papa Pete's list, folded it up, and put it in the back pocket of my jeans.

"Don't you want to read through the list?" he asked. "I'll go over it with you."

I don't like to read in front of other people, even Papa Pete. It's hard for me to read, and I'm really slow at it. And my reading problems get even worse when someone is watching me. So I try to do my reading in private. It keeps the embarrassment down that way.

"No time right now," I said to Papa Pete. "Frankie and Ashley are going to meet me downstairs to get the supplies."

"The Roll 'N Bowl party starts at six," Papa Pete said. "I'll try to be back here by seven-thirty. We'll just stay for the judging."

"Isn't Mrs. Fink going to want to stay for the whole thing?"

"Emily is coming, too," Papa Pete said. "I'll

use her as an excuse for coming home early."

At least Emily comes in handy for something, I thought. But I didn't say that out loud because I knew Papa Pete wouldn't like that.

"You go ahead and build the haunted house without me," Papa Pete said. "You're a creative boy, Hankie. You can pull this off."

I threw my arms around Papa Pete and gave him a huge hug.

"Remember this, Hankie, if you only remember one thing I ever taught you: A good brain is two things. Mushy and slimy."

"Got it, Papa Pete."

I ran out the door to meet Frankie and Ashley and search for the mushiest, slimiest brains I could find.

Just you wait, McKelty. I'll show you who's the gross-out king.

CHAPTER 11

WHEN I TOLD FRANKIE AND ASHLEY the idea for the haunted house, they couldn't get over what a great idea it was. That was, until they realized that if they were going to help me with it, they were going to have to give up trick-or-treating.

"I don't know, Zip," Frankie said. "You're asking me to turn my back on a huge bag full of candy. That candy lasts me two months."

"Candy is very bad for your dental health," I said to him. "You don't want to develop cavities, do you?"

That wasn't the best argument, I know. But understand that time was short, and we had a lot to do. I didn't have time for quality debate.

"Could I at least wear my dolphin costume in the haunted house?" Ashley asked.

I wanted to say yes, but if there's one thing I

know, it's that dolphins do not live in haunted houses.

"I'm afraid not, Ash," I said. She looked disappointed.

"Look, guys," I said, "I know this is asking a lot. And I promise that next year we'll go trick-or-treating together and get the most candy any three kids have ever gotten. But this year, I need your help. Just think about how rude and mean McKelty is. The guy needs to be put in his place."

"That's definitely true." Frankie nodded. "The big jerk shouldn't get away with that lousy attitude of his."

"Picking on little Mason like that," I added. "And making fun of Emily and Robert. They can't help it if they're geeks."

Frankie can't stand bullies. I knew my arguments were getting to him. I turned to Ashley.

"What about you, Ash?"

"Well, I suppose building the haunted house could be very creative," Ashley said.

"A great opportunity to explore your artistic side, which we all know is very strong," I agreed.

It was quiet for a long minute.

"Okay, I'm in, Zip," Frankie said.

"Me too." Ashley nodded.

Do I have great friends or what?

"If I'm giving up trick-or-treating, at least I want to be in charge of the haunted house decorations," Ashley said right away.

"And I want to be in charge of all slimy things," Frankie said.

"Unless they're slimy decorations," Ashley told him. "Then I'm in charge."

"What about a slimy eyeball that's hanging from the wall?" Frankie asked her. "Tell me, Ash, is that a decoration or is that a slimy thing?"

"Guys," I said. "Ticktock. We don't have time for this now. We have to get to the store and get going."

"Race you to Gristediano's," Frankie said. And he shot out of the lobby door like a bolt of lightning.

Gristediano's supermarket is just around the corner on Broadway, right next door to Ricardo's shoe-repair place. Since we don't have to cross any streets to get there, we are allowed to go there by ourselves. We were there before you could say "Nick McKelty is a scaredy-cat."

We grabbed the grocery basket and raced up and down the aisles. I felt like one of those contestants on a TV game show who runs up and down the aisles throwing things into a cart as fast as possible. Frankie and Ashley and I were all talking at once, because the ideas were shooting from our heads like a volcano that had just blown its top.

"We'll need grapes for eyeballs," I said.

"As the chief of all slimy things," Frankie said, "I'm not sure grapes are slimy enough for eyeballs."

"I have an idea," Ashley said. "Let's get lychee nuts. They're slimier and squishier, like a real eyeball."

Ashley's family is from China, and they eat a lot of things that I'd never heard of before. Sometimes when I eat dinner at her house, we have lychee nuts for dessert. I know they sound like they'd have a shell and be crunchy like other nuts, but actually they're soft and sweet and syrupy.

"I like the way you're thinking, Ashweena," I said. "Lychee nuts will give our haunted house an international flavor."

Unfortunately, Gristediano's didn't have lychee nuts, so we had to give up on international flavor and settle for just plain American grapes.

"Purple or green ones?" Frankie asked.

"It doesn't matter," I said, "because we're going to peel them anyway. Underneath their skin, they're all the same color."

"Wait a minute, Zip," Frankie said. "You expect me to peel grapes?"

"Yup."

"That'll happen when I change my name to Bernice."

"Frankie, you said you wanted to be in charge of all slimy things," I told him. "And a grape feels like a grape. But a peeled grape feels slimy, like an eyeball."

Frankie saluted, like I was the captain of a spaceship.

"Aye, aye, captain," Frankie said.

Ashley giggled and saluted, too.

"You lead, we follow," she said.

"Good, that's the way I like it," I answered in my best Captain Kirk voice. This was really fun. "Now, I figure we'll need two boxes of spaghetti."

"Smart thinking, captain," Frankie said. "We have to have dinner."

"Frankie, we're not eating the spaghetti. We're boiling it until it's mushy so we can make it into brains."

"Brains are good," Frankie said.

Papa Pete's words echoed in my head. Two things a brain has to be—slimy and mushy.

We raced down Aisle 9 and found the pasta section. As I was putting the spaghetti in the cart, Ashley started twirling her ponytail like she does when she's thinking.

"Captain, I have a suggestion," she said, wrapping her ponytail around her index finger. "How about we get some hot dogs and tell people they're intestines?"

"Yeah, we'll drown them in ketchup and make them into oozing intestines," Frankie added.

Their imaginations were both in full gear now, I could tell.

We got four bottles of ketchup, because we knew we'd need extra to make mummy blood.

Then we got batteries for the tape recorder. We were going to record Cheerio making scary sounds, and I certainly didn't want to take a chance on the tape recorder stopping right in the middle of a howl.

On the way out, we were lucky enough to find the last bag of rubber spiders. Ashley thought they were too ugly, but I insisted we get them.

"Ash, we'll tie some of my mom's thread around them," I said, "and we'll use a fishing pole to lower them into McKelty's hair. Wait. I don't have a fishing pole."

"My dad does," Ashley said. "We'll borrow it."

"McKelty will think he's being attacked by man-eating tarantulas," Frankie said with a laugh.

"I can't wait to see his face," I said. "We have to remember to blindfold him before he enters the chamber. Everything is twenty times scarier when you can't see."

"Boo!" somebody said from behind us.

All three of us flew three feet in the air. We were concentrating so hard on getting our supplies that we hadn't heard anyone behind us. When we turned around, we saw that it was Mrs. Fink, filling her cart with bags of fun-size candy bars. She was wearing her false teeth, which she doesn't do all the time. But I guess when you have a big date, you want all your teeth in place and reporting for duty.

"Hi, darlings," Mrs. Fink said. "Listen, I won't be home tonight when you go trick-or-treating, because I have a date with a very special someone."

My stomach flipped. I wasn't sure Papa Pete knew what he was getting himself in for.

"I've baked your grandfather a cherry strudel and an apple crumble," she whispered to me. "With an extra poppy-seed Danish thrown in for the holiday."

Obviously, when older people get crushes, there is a lot of baking involved.

"So, Hank, darling," Mrs. Fink went on. "I'll leave a big bowl of candy bars outside my door. Just help yourself, and make sure the other children do, too."

"Thanks, Mrs. Fink," I said, thinking that now Frankie could get some of his Halloween candy. "And good luck in the costume contest. I bet you guys are going to win first prize."

I wondered if she knew she was going to be the hind end of an elephant.

"I'm just looking forward to spending the evening being close to your grandfather."

Boy, they were going to be close, all right. If she only knew how close.

"Come on, Zip," Frankie said, pulling on my sleeve. "We don't have much time."

"Right. Bye, Mrs. Fink."

She waved and continued to load her cart with candy. What a nice lady, that Mrs. Fink.

At the checkout counter, the bill came to seventeen dollars and ninety-two cents. I pulled out a crisp twenty-dollar bill from my pocket. It was the one Papa Pete had given me the last time we went to a Mets game. I had been planning to use it to buy a new Mets hat. But if that twenty-dollar bill could help me get even with McKelty for being such a mean, big-mouthed jerk, I'd sacrifice a Mets hat any day. Sure, my old one had some pretty major sweat stains on it. But I ask you, who cares about a few sweat stains when crushing McKelty was so close at hand?

CHAPTER 12

TIME WASN'T EXACTLY on our side. By the time we got back to my apartment, it was seventeen minutes after five, according to Frankie's digital watch, which he'd gotten for his birthday in August. We were going to have to work fast. That was okay with me, though, because my mind was bursting with scary ideas for the haunted house.

"The first thing we have to do," I said, when we had plopped all our supplies down in the entry hall of my apartment, "is figure out where to build it."

"I think it should go right in the middle of the living room," Ashley said.

"No good, Ashweena," I answered. "It needs to be in the corner. That way, we already have two walls built."

"Good thinking, dude," Frankie said. "I

always knew you could use your head for other things than to hold up your Mets hat, which as I've said many times, I don't approve of anyway."

In case I haven't told you before, Frankie is a major Yankees fan and I'm a Mets guy, but in spite of that, we've stayed best friends. That should tell you something about how much we get along in every other area, because I love the Mets and he loves the Yankees. I mean *love* love, as in how we feel about pizza and monster movies and silver Lamborghinis.

"I say we put it in the corner by the fireplace," I suggested. "We'll use blankets to cover up the two windows there and sheets to make walls. It's got to be pitch-black inside."

"So now we go ahead and put up a haunted house?" Frankie asked. "Just like that?"

"Why not?" I said, rolling up my sleeves to get to work.

"Uh, Zip, there's a little word called parents."

"And another little word called grounded," Ashley added.

Oh, that again. Can someone please tell

me why parents are in the way of so many fun things?

I looked over at the green desk. The note Papa Pete had left for my dad was gone. To me, that meant that my dad had seen it. And he hadn't left a note saying no. These were both very good signs.

"You guys wait here," I told Frankie and Ashley. "I'll get permission."

I tiptoed into my parents' bedroom, where my dad was taking a nap in his green chair. He loves afternoon naps. He calls them power naps. They power him right into *Jeopardy*, so he can answer every question on history, geography, sports, science, and anything else involving a number or a fact. He is really smart. One thing is for sure, I certainly didn't get my brain from him.

I stood there for a minute, wondering if I should wake him to ask permission to build the haunted house. What if he said no? That was totally unacceptable. Besides, I told myself, he looked so peaceful, asleep in his chair. And it would really be a shame to wake him up. Never wake a sleeping parent unless there's blood or fire or a broken television involved. That's what I say.

I went back into the living room.

"Let's build!" I said.

"Did your dad say okay?" Ashley asked.

"Let me put it this way: He didn't say *not* okay. And that's good enough for me."

First, I grabbed the coatrack that we keep in the entry hall by the front door and dragged it into the living room. Then I unplugged the pole lamp that's next to the couch and pulled it into the middle of the floor.

"These will be great tent poles for the walls," I announced. "We'll drape sheets over them and attach the other end of the sheets to the walls with thumbtacks."

"Problem Number One," Ashley said. "Something tells me your parents won't be thrilled with us leaving holes in the wall."

"Problem solved. I'll patch up the holes afterward."

"Right. You'll do that when I change my name to Bernice," Frankie said with a laugh. "Face it, Zip. No way you're ever going to patch up these walls and not leave a complete mess."

"I'll go get some duct tape," Ashley offered. "My dad has tons of it in the bottom drawer where he keeps hammers and rope. He calls it his tool drawer, but I call it his throw-everything-in-here-when-you-don't-know-where-else-it-goes drawer."

"Bring his fishing pole, too," I hollered after her. "And some rope." I wasn't sure exactly what we would use rope for, but I knew we'd need it.

"Let's record the scary sounds while Ashley's gone," Frankie suggested.

"I like the way you're thinking," I said. "Here, Cheerio!"

There was no answer, no pitter-patter of little dog feet on the carpet.

"That's strange," I told Frankie. "Cheerio always comes when I call him."

"He probably can't hear you over your dad's snoring," Frankie said. "Hey, Zip, I was going to ask you anyway. Would it be okay if I recorded the sounds instead of Cheerio?"

"Can you howl?"

"Check this out."

Frankie let loose with what has to be the strangest sound I've ever heard come out of a human mouth. It started out like a creaking door blowing in the wind, then turned into a creepy ghostly moan, and ended in a truly scary wolflike howl.

"Where have you been keeping that?" I asked him. I mean, you know a guy your whole life, you think you know all the sound effects he can do. Car engines, helicopters, sirens, explosions, the usual. Then he pulls out something amazing like that crazed wolf howl, and you have to wonder what else you don't know about him.

"What was that?" said a voice that sounded very much like my sister Emily's. That's because it was Emily's.

I turned around and there she was, standing with her hands on her hips and her pet iguana, Katherine, on her shoulder. "Whoever made that awful screech should know that you scared poor Katherine. Look. She's shaking."

I looked at Katherine. She was giving me the big stink eye as she flicked her lizardy tongue from side to side. She didn't look scared to me. Just ugly.

"That sound reached quite a high decibel

level," Robert chimed in. He had followed Emily out into the living room. I noticed that his voice sounded especially nasal. Maybe he was allergic to his pus costume. Without grossing you out entirely, let's just say Robert has a major, no really, a *major* sinus problem. It's like he's got a nasal flood going on all the time. I bet the guy who invented Kleenex could buy his own baseball team just from the money he's made off Robert's nose river.

"The iguana is extremely sensitive to sudden changes in the audio environment," Robert went on, as if anyone besides Emily cared.

"Thanks for the science lesson, little man," I said, nudging him aside. "But unfortunately we don't have time right now for an in-depth discussion of iguana feelings. We're on a deadline."

Before I could stop her, Miss Know-It-All and her shoulder lizard were poking around in our construction site.

"What's going on here?" Emily asked.

"Stuff that wouldn't interest you."

"Mom and Dad are going to kill you," Emily said. "Do you want to explain what the coatrack and the lamp are doing in the middle of the living room?"

"No."

"Hank, you're making a horrible mess."

"Emily, I don't need criticism right now," I said. "If you're not part of the solution, you're part of the problem."

Papa Pete always says that to me, and it felt great to have the chance to say it myself.

"We're building a haunted house," Frankie told Emily and Robert. "It was all Hank's idea. Cool, huh?"

"You're going to be grounded until next Halloween," Emily said in her usual positive, helpful, creative tone of voice. "You never learn, do you?"

Katherine hissed at me. She copies everything that Emily does, and when Emily gets mad, Katherine does, too.

"Calm yourself, Kathy," I hissed back at her. "You're prettier when you smile."

"Please don't make fun of Katherine's looks," Emily whispered. "Her feelings get hurt very easily."

In case you hadn't noticed, my sister is

extremely tuned in to the psychology of the female iguana. I believe that because she's half iguana herself. Don't ask me which half.

"For your information, Lizard Girl," I said to Emily, "I am doing this for you, too."

Emily pointed her index finger at me, just the way my dad does when he gets mad.

"You're making a total mess of our house, and you claim it's for me? Explain please."

"We're building this whole haunted house to scare only one special guest. And that would be his bullyness, Nick the Tick McKelty."

"He's coming here?" Emily's mouth flew open. Katherine's did, too.

"At seven-thirty on the dot."

"Well, let's get going," Emily said, grabbing the coatrack. "Where do you want this baby?"

"Boy, you changed your tune awful quick. I thought you just said I was going to get grounded for this."

"That was before I realized how important your plan is for the benefit of all mankind," Emily said. "Getting even with Nick McKelty should be the number-one priority of the human race."

"Emily," Robert said, "much as we'd like to help, we don't have time. We have to meet your grandfather at Mrs. Fink's in ten minutes."

"Oh, you're right, Robert. Our costumes aren't even ready yet."

"Sure they are, dudes," Frankie said. "I saw you in the parade. Your costumes are all done."

"We're not wearing those costumes," Emily said.

"You're telling me you're giving up on the flu-germ concept?" Frankie said. "What's Halloween without a pus pocket?"

"That Nick McKelty was so mean that we don't want to take a chance of being made fun of again," Robert said. "So we've made new costumes. I'm going as a knight."

"No way," I said.

"Yes, way," Robert answered. "I used two-and-a-half rolls of tinfoil to make my armor and shield."

"And I'm going as a princess," Emily said.

"You can't!" I protested. "There are millions of princesses on the streets. But only one flu germ—and that's you, Emily."

"Besides, you should be yourself," Frankie added.

"Trust me, Emily, deep inside you're much more of a pus pocket than a princess," I chimed in, just to be annoying.

"Do you really think so, Hank?" Emily asked. She sounded really happy with my observation. Even Katherine seemed to be flashing me the old iguana grin.

"Absolutely. Now you march yourself right back in your room and put on the right costume. You too, Robert. Get in there and think pus."

"I don't know, Hank. Let me ask Katherine what she thinks. What do you think I should wear?" Emily whispered to Old Kath.

My sister is undoubtedly the only person in the world strange enough to ask a lizard for fashion advice. And what's even stranger is that we all stood there waiting for the answer.

"What'd she say?" I finally blurted out.

"Katherine's still thinking about it," Emily said. "We'll let you know what we decide."

"You do that, Em," I said. "Now if you three will excuse us, we have a house to haunt."

Just then, Ashley came running into the

apartment, carrying an armful of supplies—duct tape, rope, a hammer, a fishing pole, and a big white plastic skeleton.

"Whoa, where'd that dude come from?" Frankie said. "He looks like he could use a meal."

"My dad used him in medical school to study bones and stuff," Ashley told us. "He lives in the hall closet behind a box of plastic body organs. There's a heart in there, a couple of lungs, a liver, and something that's yellow."

"Well, are we going to stand here discussing body parts, or are we going to build a haunted house?" I said.

That needed no answer. There was work to be done, and I, for one, couldn't wait to start.

CHAPTER 13

THE TEN COOLEST THINGS
WE PUT IN OUR HAUNTED HOUSE

Can you guess who came up with these plans for our haunted house? Try to figure it out as you read each one. Good luck. I hope you get all ten right.

1. We hung the black light on the skeleton's ribs, so the entire bony dude glowed a creepy whitish, purplish color.
2. We tied all the rubber spiders onto Ashley's dad's fishing pole and hung it in the corner, so when people walked by, we could drop the spiders into their hair. That would make the hair on their necks stand at attention.
3. We recorded Frankie's scary howl into a tape recorder. Then we slowed the tape recorder

down so when we played it back, the howls turned into spine-chilling shrieks.

4. We peeled grapes so they had the perfect texture for eyeballs and put them in a bowl of slimy egg whites as if the eyeballs had just spewed their gooey insides into the bowl.

5. We made a human brain by boiling spaghetti noodles until they were mushy and mixing them with Marshmallow Fluff so the brain would stick to kids' fingers when they touched it. Nobody wants to walk around with gray matter stuck to their fingers.

6. We lined my old Mets hat with Saran Wrap and put the brain mixture in it. When kids stuck their hands in that hat, they would think someone took their hat off and their brain came with it. (I'm even grossing myself out now.)

7. We made a ghost out of Emily's bedsheet, and then we put a fan under it, so it would billow out and look like it was about to take off and fly around the room.

8. We went through three large economy-size

bottles of ketchup, covering most anything you can think of with fake ketchup blood—including a roasting fork, gauze bandages, and an old undershirt of my dad's.

9. We saved the last bottle of ketchup to add a bloody spot to the ghost's chest area, where its heart would have been.

10. We put Ashley's head through the cardboard from my Italian table costume. Then we squirted Ashley's cheeks with ketchup and threw a napkin over her head. We gave her a flashlight to light up under her chin whenever someone uncovered her head.

Answer Key
1. Hank***
2. Hank***
3. Hank***
4. Hank*** (although Ashley peeled the grapes)
5. Hank***
6. Hank***
7. Hank*** (Frankie pulled the sheet off the bed)
8. Hank***

9. Hank***
10. Hank***

*** I hope it doesn't seem like bragging for me to take the credit for all the ideas, but I felt really proud of them. It's not every day that I actually get to say I'm proud of my brain. So excuse me for getting a little excited.

CHAPTER 14

WHEN WE FINISHED, it was six-forty-eight, according to Frankie's watch. Boy, when you're inspired, you work fast. It's like your hands and feet are attached to a million bodies all working together.

We were so focused on putting the haunted house together that we didn't even see Emily and Robert leave. They just shouted good-bye, and not one of us even popped our heads outside the sheets to see them in their costumes or to find out which costumes they were wearing. The best news was that I thought I heard my dad shout good-bye along with them. That meant that either I wasn't going to get grounded at all, or at least not until he came back. I had a feeling Emily talked him into letting us make the haunted house. She becomes a great sister sometimes when I least expect it. I can't figure out girls.

As we looked at what we had built, we felt really proud. The haunted house took up almost half of our living room. True, it didn't look like much on the outside, just a bunch of sheets and bedspreads strung together. The inside, though, was full of scary, fun things. Ashley made a sign that said: "ENTER AT YOUR OWN RISK." We hung it up over the door flap. Then we turned on the black light inside the skeleton dude. It made the sheets glow like those iridescent fish that live at the bottom of the ocean. When we dimmed the living-room lights, our little haunted house looked like it was a floating alien spaceship. Or at least, that's what it looked like to us.

"McKelty is going to be scared out of his mind," I said.

"That's if everything works right," Frankie said. "Don't forget, Zip, it's never been tested."

"We should have some kids test it out before McKelty gets here," Ashley said.

"There's not much time for that now," I said. "Who lives close?"

"Heather Payne lives on 78th Street and West End Avenue," Frankie said.

Ashley and I both shot him a look that

said "Since When Are You Hanging Out with Heather Payne, the Girl Who Cries if She Doesn't Get an A-Plus on Every Extra-Credit Project She Does?" (Which, by the way, is all of them.)

Frankie could read our minds, because he added quickly, "Hey, don't even go there, guys. We did a science project together. That's all. Remember, we created an earthworm farm?"

"Right. I remember now." I snickered. "The Biggle Wiggle Worm Wigwam."

Ashley and I both cracked up. Frankie wasn't so amused.

"Listen, man, the name was *her* idea," he said. "I wanted to call it something cool like the Worm Crib. But she flat out refused."

"Well, since you and Heather are such close personal Biggle Wiggle Worm Wigwam buddies, why don't you call her and tell her to come here as soon as possible?" I suggested.

"Don't say I never did anything for you, Zip," Frankie said, getting up and heading toward the kitchen.

"And Luke Whitman lives around the corner on Amsterdam Avenue!" I shouted out. "While you're at it, call him, too."

"Eeww, he's so gross," Ashley moaned. "The other day, I saw him take a used piece of American cheese out of the trash, smell it, and then eat it."

Frankie disappeared into the kitchen to use the phone.

"Do you think two kids are enough to test everything out?" I asked Ashley.

"It better be," she said. "It's what we have."

At exactly six-fifty-three, the front door flew open. I was hoping it was Heather or Luke, but no, it was just my mom.

"I didn't miss any of the trick-or-treaters yet, did I?" she said, flinging off her jacket with the big, green pickle embroidered on the back. She had those jackets made last year as a holiday present for all the people who work at the Crunchy Pickle. "I made a special batch of prune taffy to give out tonight."

"Wow, Mrs. Z.," Frankie said. "Don't let that out or every kid on the Upper West Side will be lined up around the block."

"Do you really think so?" my mom asked.

"Prune taffy. The name alone has my mouth watering," Ashley said.

"I knew it'd be a crowd-pleaser," my mom said. She just doesn't get it that not everyone is as thrilled with prunes as she is. "And I wrapped each one individually in cellophane with a little orange-and-black ribbon. Don't they look sweet?"

I was waiting for her to notice the living room. It took her a minute, I guess because her head was still in her prune-taffy ribbons, but when she finally looked around, her eyes almost fell out of her head.

"Hank, where did you put our living room?"

"It doesn't exist any longer, Mom. You have entered the chamber of horrors."

"That's my bedspread," she said, pointing to the wall we had made for the haunted house.

"Your bedspread had the honor of being selected from all the bedspreads in the house to form the front wall of the scariest place on the planet," I told her.

"Hank, honey," she said, "this is so creative."

You have to meet my mom someday. She is really a lot of fun. She almost never gets mad when I make a mess, because she says creativity and neatness don't go together. It's like she can see deep inside me.

"Vlady," she called out, running into the entry hall. "Bring the platters of prune taffy and come see what Hank and his friends have made!"

Vladimir Olefski has worked for my mom at the Crunchy Pickle ever since he came to New York from his home in Russia. He is known for making the best sandwiches on all of the West Side because he stacks them really high with meat and then adds a special zingy red sauce that the customers love so much, they write my mom letters about it.

Vlady came into the living room. He was carrying two big trays of the prune taffy. It looked like hunks of dark brown shoe leather topped with little pieces of yellow fuzz. You don't even want to know what the yellow fuzz was, because it was probably something weird like dandelion pollen. From looking at that platter, I had a pretty strong feeling that we were going to have plenty of prune taffy left over.

"Hello, little ones," Vlady said in his thick Russian accent.

You have to understand that everyone is a "little one" compared to Vlady. He's so big, I didn't think he was going to fit through the haunted house flap door. But he didn't have to, because he looked right over the top of the sheets and stared down at what we had created.

"This look like Babushka's place back home in Poltava," he said.

"What's a babushka?" Ashley asked him.

"Not what. Who. *Babushka* is Russian word for 'grandmother.' "

"Your grandma lives in a haunted house?" Frankie said. "Wow. She must cool."

"That stuff," Vlady said, pointing to the mushy brains in the baseball cap. "That look like Babushka's breakfast porridge," he said.

I could see Ashley trying not to laugh.

"And that guy," he said, pointing to the skeleton, "remind me of Olga, our cow back in Poltava. There was no grass in our meadow so she was . . . how you say . . . skinny like a toothpick. Maybe two toothpicks."

That did it. We cracked up. Vlady didn't laugh, though. I guess he was still thinking about Olga the Cow.

"What you need is vampire," Vlady said. "There are many vampires in my country. My grandfather Boris, for example."

"You're kidding! Your grandfather was a real vampire?" I asked him.

"We didn't know for sure," Vlady said. "But we never let him kiss us on neck, just in case."

Vlady's bright blue eyes were twinkling. I wasn't sure if he was kidding us or if he was just misty, thinking of his grandpa.

"Well, much as we'd love to have a vampire, there's no time for that now," Ashley said. "We're expecting the first visitors to the haunted house here any second."

Vlady dropped off the platters of prune taffy in the kitchen and said good-bye.

Ashley, Frankie, and I waited by the door. Where was that Heather Payne? It was only a half hour until McKelty was supposed to arrive. And we still had to check out the haunted house to see if it was ready for that one incredible moment when Nick the Tick would wet his pants and never show his face in public again.

The doorbell rang.

"It's showtime," I said. "Ditch the lights."

Ashley and Frankie took their places inside the haunted house. As I crept to the door, I could hear my own heart pounding.

I opened the door, and it was . . .

CHAPTER 15

DON'T GET EXCITED. It was just my dad.

"Why is it so dark in here?" he asked.

"Dad," I tried to explain, "it has to be dark. We're just about to open the haunted house. See, we decided to build it and . . ."

"I know," he interrupted. "Emily told me all about it. Nevertheless, I need the lights on."

"But lights and ghosty things just don't go together."

"Do you see this?" my dad said, holding up a white plastic bag. "It contains the brand-new edition of the *New York Times Big Book of Crossword Puzzles*. I have been waiting for this to come out for two months. Now tell me, Hank, how can I read the clues in the dark?"

"Dad, I can't believe you're thinking about crossword puzzles tonight. This is H-A-L-L-O-W-E-E-N. As in an eight-letter word for scary fun holiday."

"Hank, Halloween has nine letters."

Is my dad a total spelling machine, or what?

I tried to explain that we needed the living room totally dark for the haunted house, but my dad just wasn't in a listening mood. Luckily, my mom must have overheard our conversation. She waltzed into the living room, hooked her arm in his, and flashed me this little wink she does with her left eye. Maybe it's her right eye. You know I can't tell the difference. It didn't matter, because that wink meant she had a plan.

"Come in the kitchen, Stanley," she said. "I've got a nice cauliflower-and-beet stew for us—and your favorite mechanical pencil is just waiting for you in the kitchen."

"Sounds like my kind of evening," my dad said. Without even a backward glance, my mom waltzed into the kitchen with my dad.

Randi Zipzer, you are a rock star!

I didn't even have time to say thanks because there it was again. The doorbell. This time I knew it had to be Heather Payne. Or maybe Luke Whitman.

Oh boy, the fun was about to start!

CHAPTER 16

"COMING!" I heard myself holler.

Oh no. That voice wouldn't do. It sounded exactly like me.

"Coming!" I repeated in my deepest, creepiest voice. "The spirits are preparing to let you in!"

Oh yes. That was much better.

Ashley dashed back into the haunted house and stuck her head through the hole in the cardboard. I was on my way to the front door but stopped halfway. I turned, ran back to Ashley, and blasted a few last-minute squirts of ketchup on her cheeks. If I didn't know better myself, I would've thought she was nothing more than a bloody head on a plate. I threw the napkin over her head.

"Hank, the flashlight!" she whispered.

I handed it to her. Frankie took his position

at the spider fishing pole and flashed me the okay sign. I went to the front door, turning on the tape recorder just before I got there. The apartment echoed with the sounds of Frankie's moans and groans.

I opened the door just a crack.

"Do you dare enter the chamber of fear?" I growled.

There was silence on the other side of the door, so I went for it even more.

"Come in at your own risk. Ghosts and goblins await you." Then I let out a really crazed laugh.

"Mommy!" a little voice cried. "I want to go home!"

That didn't sound like Heather Payne. And it sure didn't sound like Luke Whitman. Besides, there was no bad smell coming through the crack in the door. Luke doesn't like to take baths too often.

"Tyler," a woman's voice said. "It's your friend Hank. He's just pretending to be scary."

"No, he isn't," said the little voice. "He's really scary, and I'm scared of all scary things!"

Oh no. It was Tyler King, the five-year-old

who lives on our floor. He's the last person on earth I'd want to scare. I flicked on the lights and opened the door all the way.

"See, Tyler, it's just me, Hank!" I said.

"I'm not Tyler," he whimpered, still clinging onto his mom's skirt. "I'm Spider-Man."

Of course he was. He wears his Spider-Man Halloween costume three hundred and sixty-five days a year. I get that because when I was five, I wore my Aquaman costume all the time. Aquaman could swim through water faster than a submarine. I'd splash water all over myself so I'd look like I just swam out of the ocean, too. My mom spent a year with a towel hooked to her belt because every time she turned her back, I had soaked myself. When he was little, Frankie was obsessed with Luke Skywalker. You had to be very careful around him because he would constantly poke you in the butt with his light saber. It was a great day for my rear end when he finally outgrew that.

"Listen, Spider-Man," I said to Tyler. "How would you like a piece of prune taffy?"

"Ick," he said. "I want M&M's. With peanuts."

"You're out of luck, buddy," I said. "This isn't exactly the best trick-or-treat stop in the building."

"Try my apartment," Frankie called out. "Apartment 4B. My mom's got lots of those little bags of M&M's."

"Are there ghosts there, too?" Tyler asked.

"No, man. Just my brother Otis. The only thing scary about him is his breath."

Tyler turned and ran toward the elevator. As he and his mom got in, I heard footsteps coming out. I slammed the door fast, ditched the lights, and got back to my position just in time.

Ding-dong.

"Do you dare enter the chamber of fear?" I growled, opening the door a crack.

"Of course I do. Why do you think I came over on a homework night?"

Oh yes, that could only be the voice of Heather Payne. Leave it to her to bring up homework on the most fun night of the year.

I opened the door and Heather came in. She was dressed as an old woman in a gray skirt with gray shoes and gray glasses and gray hair.

Don't tell me! Was Heather Payne trick-or-

treating as Ms. Adolf?

That might have been one of the scariest things I'd ever seen in my life. Who goes dressed up as their teacher, especially if their teacher is Ms. Adolf? It's just not normal, I tell you.

"So where is this haunted house?" Heather said, tapping her gray shoe impatiently. "I don't have all night, you know. We have a social studies report due next week, and I want to get an early start on it."

"Follow me . . . if your nerves can handle it," I said.

You have to give me credit for continuing to be scary. It wasn't easy when you had a fun-pooper like Heather Payne on your hands.

I led Heather down the hall and into the living room. If it had been anyone else, I probably would have taken her hand, but the thought of holding hands with Heather Payne . . . was . . . well, let's not even go there.

When we reached the haunted house, I held up the door flap.

"You may enter," I said. "I hope you come out alive."

Heather went in. I followed her. Frankie was

at the spider fishing pole. I could barely see him because he was dressed all in black so his clothes would blend into the darkness. I took my place behind the table with all the gooey things.

"Wander as you wish," I whispered. "But beware of ghosts. The spirits are restless tonight."

First, Heather went to the skeleton with the black light inside his chest. She reached out to touch him. *Plop!* His arm fell off. We hadn't planned that, but I thought it was a nice touch. Heather didn't flinch, though. She just reached down and picked up the arm.

"Your skeleton's broken," she said. "Try super glue. It's very adhesive."

Mental note to self: Glue on skeleton arms BEFORE McKelty arrives.

Next, Heather went to where Ashley's head was sticking through the table.

"Pull the napkin off," I whispered. "And be afraid. Very afraid."

Heather pulled the napkin off, and Ashley let out a high-pitched scream as she switched on the flashlight under her chin.

"Hi, Ashley," Heather said. "You got some

ketchup on your face. You smell like a hamburger."

Mental note to self: Add more ketchup. Work on Ashley's screaming technique.

Then Heather went to the table with the icky gooey stuff. She stuck her hand into the bowl with the peeled grapes floating in egg whites.

"These are the eyeballs of Frankenstein," I whispered.

Heather swished the grapes around with her fingers. I was hoping for her to vomit or at least spit up a little. Instead, all she did was wipe her hand on her Ms. Adolf-y skirt.

"Egg whites," she said. "My mother says we shouldn't waste food. If I hadn't already touched them, you could use them in a nice nutritious omelet."

This girl sure knew how to have fun. I picked up my Mets cap that held the spaghetti and Marshmallow Fluff brain mixture.

"These are Dracula's brains," I whispered. "They have been preserved for two hundred years. He asks that you touch them."

Heather stuck her hand in my baseball cap.

"You should really have some moist

towelettes for people to wipe their hands on," she commented. "I'm sure this concoction will stain the furniture."

Moist towelettes? Give me a break!

Mental note to self: Heather Payne has the perfect name because she IS a pain with zero sense of fun. Correction. Make that minus zero.

For what I was hoping would be the big finish, I guided Heather over to the dangling spiders. As she stood there, Frankie lowered the spiders down onto her head. Well, he was aiming for her head, that is. He missed, and the spiders shot right by her and dropped all the way to the ground until they just sat there on her gray Ms. Adolf-y shoe.

"I saw those spiders in the market," Heather said. "They were three for eighty-nine cents, which would be twenty-nine point six cents each. Twenty-seven if you round up."

She was doing math problems in our haunted house! I couldn't believe it!

Mental note to self: Never invite Heather Payne again. To anything. Anywhere. Anytime. Ever again.

CHAPTER 17

WHEN SHE WAS FINISHED with the haunted house, we gave Heather Payne some prune-taffy treats. Actually, we gave her *a whole lot* of prune-taffy treats. And you're not going to believe this, but she was really happy to get them. That's how weird she is.

"This looks delicious and healthy," she said when we stuffed a fistful of the wrapped shoe leather chunks into her hand. "Not like all those sugary candies other people give out."

Sugary candies! It was like Ms. Adolf was inhabiting Heather's body!

Wait! Could Heather Payne possibly be a clone of Ms. Adolf?

I shuddered to think that there might be more than one Ms. Adolf in the world. One Ms. Adolf was quite enough. Way more than enough.

As quickly as we could, we sent Heather on her way. After all, the girl wanted to get a head start on her social studies report. Plus, she was a total flop in the fun department. We did thank her for coming out on a school night. Politeness is important, especially when you're running a haunted house.

We had to hurry to set up for Luke Whitman. The first outing of the haunted house had been pretty disappointing. We only had one more chance to get it right before McKelty arrived.

Frankie picked up the arm that had fallen off the skeleton.

"Okay, captain, what do we do about this skinny dude's arm?" he asked, waving it under my nose. "Or should I say lack of one?"

I propped the arm bone up so it looked like it was attached to the skeleton again.

"At first I thought we should glue it back. But now I say we just leave it there," I said. "I think it's cool when it falls off like it's rotten. Scarier even than when it was attached."

"It didn't seem to scare Heather Payne," Frankie pointed out.

"Heather Payne wouldn't know a scary thing

if it landed right on her. And speaking of things landing on her—Frankie, you have to work on your aim. The spiders have got to land bull's-eye on top of the victim's head."

"Cut me a break, Zip. I'm new to this fishing thing."

"And, Ash," I called in to her. "You've got to scream like you mean it. Really let it rip."

"Like this?" Ashley asked, and let out a bloodcurdling scream that was so loud, I thought her tonsils were going to blow out of her throat and land on the fireplace mantel. She let out so much air, it fogged up her glasses.

"*Shhhh,*" I whispered. "I hear footsteps. "Places, everyone. I want everything to work perfectly this time."

Ding-dong.

I opened the door a crack and saw Luke Whitman. Actually, I smelled him first, then saw him. He was all wrapped up like an Egyptian mummy, except instead of using ancient cloth, he had used toilet paper. His arms and legs and body were completely wrapped up. Wow, he had probably used ten rolls of toilet paper. I hoped no one in his house had to go to the bathroom real bad that night.

"Enter our chamber of fear, if you dare," I said, clicking the tape recorder on as Luke entered. I expected the living room to fill with Frankie's horrible moans. Mistake Number One. After Heather had left, I must have forgotten to rewind the tape back to the beginning, so instead of moans, the living room echoed with an even more hideous sound. It was Emily, singing one of her made-up lullabies to Katherine. It must have been on the tape before we recorded over it.

I won't make you sick by repeating the whole song. Let me just tell you that it started like this, and got even worse as it went along.

Good night, little Kathy.
It's after your bathy.
Oh, lizard, rest your head
In your comfy lizard bed . . .

And if the words weren't bad enough, Emily's voice sounded like an amped-up police siren with a bad cold.

"Those are scary sounds, dude," Luke Whitman said. "Sends chills down my spine big-time."

Then he started to wail in a voice that sounded even worse than Emily's. I could hear Katherine hissing from the bedroom, which only added to the hair-raising sound track that was going on in our living room.

Oh, it got even better from there. Luke was the perfect test for our haunted house. He was born to be grossed out.

First of all, he loved it when the skeleton's arm bone detached in his hand.

"Wow, decay," Luke said. "I love decay. I don't brush for that very reason."

And when it came to the eyeball grapes in egg whites, not only did he stick both hands in and feel them, he ate a couple, too.

"Excellent eyeball goo, dude," he said.

After he touched the brains, he licked the goopy crud off his fingers and then pretended to barf. At least I think he was pretending. Not to gross you out, but the sound effects were pretty realistic. So I pushed the record button on the tape recorder to get them on tape. They would come in handy later.

The best was when Luke pulled the napkin off of Ashley's head and saw her ketchup-splattered face.

"She's been attacked by zombies!" he shouted, like he had just seen a herd of killer zombies himself. "The living dead!"

Ashley let out a bloodcurdling scream. Then Luke screamed. Then Ashley screamed. Then Luke. Then Ashley. Then Luke. I thought they were both going to pass out.

"This is the most fun I've ever had," Luke said.

I was amazed that he could even talk. You'd think that he would have been really weak after that screamfest. He must have been really pumped up, because when Frankie lowered the spiders onto his head, he jumped five feet in the air.

"Man-eating giant tarantulas!" he yelled. "I'm poisoned."

Frankie dangled the spiders over Luke's head, and Luke batted at them in the dark room. He battled with the spiders so much that his mummy wrapping started to unravel. Pretty soon, he was dragging a giant tail of toilet paper behind him.

"My mummy skin!" he shrieked. "I'm

coming apart! Help! I'm turning to dust."

Luke continued to shriek as he ran out of the haunted house, out of our living room, and out the door of our apartment.

"So long, dudes," he screamed. "Great event!"

As he rode down in the elevator, we could hear his voice in the shaft yelling, "Help! I'm dissolving."

That guy just couldn't turn it off.

When he was gone, Frankie and Ashley came flying out of the haunted house.

We couldn't stop laughing and high-fiving one another.

Wow. Had we ever pulled it off! We were a giant hit. A complete success. We had passed the Luke Whitman test. We had made a totally cool, totally scary, totally terrifying, totally fun haunted house.

The trap was ready.

We were set to go.

Now all we needed was a victim.

Bring on Nick McKelty!

CHAPTER 18

WE TOOK OUR PLACES AND WAITED. It was so quiet in the living room, you could hear the *blip blip blip* of my dad's laptop computer from his bedroom.

He must be getting an e-mail from one of his crossword-puzzle buddies.

Those guys are such crossword fanatics, they actually send each other clues over the Internet.

Hey, I have a clue. What is a seven-letter word for a scared bully?

M-c-K-E-L-T-Y.

Wow, Hankster. I think you even spelled his name right. That's a first.

"Hank," my mom called out from the kitchen. "Come in here."

"Not now, Mom," I hollered back. "We're waiting for Nick McKelty."

"It's important, Hank. Come here now."

That wasn't her usual tone of voice. That was her I-mean-business voice. I told Frankie and Ashley not to move a muscle, and hurried into the kitchen.

"What's up, Mom? I'm kind of busy right now."

"Have you seen Cheerio?" she asked.

"Maybe he's sleeping in my room," I said.

Cheerio likes sleeping in my room best. He never sleeps in Emily's room because he's not a big fan of Katherine flicking her nasty gray tongue out at him. It's one of the many things he and I have in common, along with a love of juicy steaks, large ears, and a fear of the squirrels in Central Park. Maybe all these things we have in common are what make us close. Anyway, I think he likes sleeping in my room best because everything smells like me—not that I smell so great, but that the smell reminds him of me. Like sometimes, if I toss my shirt on the floor when I go to take a shower, when I come back he's all curled up on it, fast asleep. A boy and his dog. You can't beat that.

"I looked in your room," my mom said. "And in our room. And under the beds and in the bathroom and in the closets, too. He's not here, Hank."

Come to think of it, I hadn't seen Cheerio since we started to build the haunted house. I remembered that he hadn't come when I called him. That wasn't like him. My heart started to pound in my chest.

"I'll look outside in the hall," I said, and bolted for the front door.

"Is McKelty here yet?" Ashley called as I dashed past the haunted house. I didn't even stop to answer.

I ran out into our hallway and looked around. Mrs. Fink's door was locked up tight, which made sense because she was at the bowling alley with Papa Pete. A big bowl of candy bars sat on a TV tray that she had left outside her door. I knocked on apartment 10C, Mrs. King's door. When she opened it, she was holding a bowl of candy. I'm sure she thought I was going to be a trick-or-treater.

"Mrs. King, have you seen Cheerio?" I asked. "He's missing."

"Why no, Hank," she answered. "Tyler and I just came back from trick-or-treating in the building. I didn't see him anywhere."

"Thanks, Mrs. King," I said. "I have to go now."

I looked frantically around every inch of the hall, including the dark corners near the elevator. Cheerio definitely wasn't there.

I practically flew back into the apartment. By that time, Ashley and Frankie had come out of the haunted house, and my parents were in the living room.

"Cheerio's gone," I said. I could hardly believe my own words.

"When did you see him last?" my mom asked.

"When I came home from school with Papa Pete," I said. "I gave him a big tummy scratch."

"And since then, did you leave the front door open?" my dad asked.

"Of course not, Dad. Well, I don't know. We were just so busy putting everything together. Maybe I did forget to close the door. Oh man, how stupid can I be?"

"When was the last time you heard him in the house?" My dad's forehead was all crinkled up. My mom calls those his worry lines.

"I'm not sure, Dad. I didn't notice. I just don't know."

"I'll go look for him on the street," my dad said, throwing on his overcoat.

"And I'll call the animal shelter," my mom said, going into the kitchen.

I felt terrible, like someone had punched me in the stomach.

"I'm sorry, dude," Frankie said, laying aside the fishing pole and putting his hand on my shoulder.

"He'll turn up, Hank," Ashley said. "Cheerio wouldn't run away. He loves it here."

"He loves it here on normal days," I said. "But imagine what today must have been like for him. Dark rooms, black lights, scary sounds, skeleton bones, people screaming. Poor little guy must have been scared out of his mind."

I remembered that Papa Pete had said how much Halloween scared dogs. Why hadn't I listened to what he was telling me?

"I'll go look on the other floors," I said. I had a lump in my throat as big as one of those prune-taffy globs.

"We'll help," Ashley offered.

"What should we do about the haunted house, Zip?" Frankie asked. "And McKelty? He's supposed to be here in fifteen minutes."

"I don't care about McKelty anymore," I said. "If I hadn't been so focused on getting even with him, I would have paid more attention to what was going on. I would have looked out for Cheerio."

"You can't blame yourself," Ashley said, giving me a hug.

But I did blame myself—and my stupid brain that can't do two things at once. I should have been able to build the haunted house *and* watch out for my dog, don't you think?

I left the apartment and headed for the stairway.

Cheerio, where are you, boy? Come home.

CHAPTER 19

FRANKIE, ASHLEY, AND I searched up and down every single floor of our apartment building. Kids swarmed all over the halls, dressed as pirates and princesses and skeletons and fairy godmothers. There were jack-o'-lanterns near the doors that glowed with candlelight and smelled like pumpkin pie. All of the children were knocking on doors and grabbing handfuls of candy, and all the grown-ups were smiling and saying, "And what are you supposed to be?"

They were happy. Not me. I was miserable.

We split up and went to each apartment. We asked everyone if they had seen Cheerio. No one had.

My dad came back in from the street. He had asked people up and down the block if they had seen a brown dachshund with a red collar.

No one had.

My mom came in from the kitchen. She had talked to the West Side Animal Shelter and asked if they had a dachshund of any kind.

They didn't.

We gathered back in our apartment. Frankie and Ashley didn't know what to say. I mean, what can you say to someone whose dog has disappeared?

I heard the sounds of laughter echoing from all over the building. I saw our haunted house just waiting to be enjoyed.

And I wondered how such a happy night could have turned so sad.

CHAPTER 20

TEN THINGS I MISS ABOUT CHEERIO ALREADY

1. His brown eyes that look at me and say, "Hank, buddy, I can't believe you're not sharing your steak with me!"
2. His long hot-dog body that is so close to the ground, he could walk under my bed on his tiptoes if he wanted to.
3. The way he is absolutely positive he's a big dog even though he's not.
4. His floppy ears that perk up when he hears the *SpongeBob SquarePants* theme song on TV.
5. The way his bottom teeth stick out over his top teeth to make him look like he's smiling at you upside down.
6. The way he looks like a Cheerio when he

chases his tail and spins in a circle.

7. The way he snarls at Katherine when she's having a hissy fit.

8. The way he snarls at Katherine when she *isn't* having a hissy fit.

9. The way his little claws click on the linoleum when he's cruising around the kitchen looking for leftovers, which is most of the time.

10. The way he drops his favorite golf ball at my feet and looks at me as if to say, "Any chance for a catch, pal?"

11. A million billion other things that are all so cute if I mention them I swear I'll start to cry.

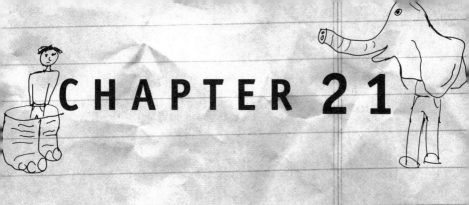

CHAPTER 21

WE JUST SAT THERE on the couch, my mom, my dad, and me, feeling like a black cloud had blown into our apartment and was raining on our heads. I have to hand it to Frankie and Ashley. They stayed right there by my side, which is hard to do when someone is as sad as I was.

The doorbell rang.

"It's probably more trick-or-treaters," my mom said.

"Let's just turn out the lights and pretend we're not home," I said. The last thing I wanted was noisy little pirates swaggering through our door. I know that sounds horrible and grumpy, but all I could think about was Cheerio, out there on the street somewhere, lost and scared and alone.

"That's not right, Hank," my mom said.

"Frankie, answer the door please and give the children a piece of prune taffy. We shouldn't deprive them."

I could tell Frankie didn't want to be the one handing out the prune taffy. Trying to give away my mom's "treats" is a really tough job. Last year when I was handing out her curried fig roll-ups, which looked even more like shoe leather than the prune taffy, one little boy actually cried.

Frankie is too nice a kid to say no to anyone's mom, especially mine, who is like his second mom anyway. He took a piece of prune taffy off the platter and opened the door. I was surprised to see that it wasn't one of the kids from our building. It was Ryan Shimozato, who is probably the coolest kid in our class—after Frankie, that is. He was dressed like a goalie for the New York Rangers.

"Hey, Frankie," Ryan said. "I just saw Luke Whitman on the street. He says you guys have an extremely excellent haunted house. Can I see it?"

"I don't know, dude," Frankie said. "This isn't exactly a good time. The ghosts are kind of resting."

"I heard you have a real zombie," Ryan said. He wasn't taking no for an answer.

Frankie didn't know what to say, so Ashley got up and went to the door. She is very good at handling business matters.

"I'm sorry, Ryan," she said. "But the haunted house is closed for repairs right now."

"Too bad," he said. "I wanted one of those Frankenstein eyeballs."

"They rolled themselves into the closet," said Ashley. "Maybe try again next Halloween. And thanks for your interest."

Wow, she was smooth. Ryan turned to leave.

"Oh, I almost forgot," Ryan said, just before Ashley shut the door. "McKelty said to tell you guys he'd be here later. He said he had to meet the governor of New York at the bowling alley first."

"Right," said Frankie. "And my name is Bernice. Like I'm sure the governor of New York wants to hang out with Nick McKelty."

McKelty exaggerates everything. We call it the McKelty factor—truth times a hundred. Instead of meeting the governor, I bet he was really washing dishes for his dad's party. But it didn't matter to me. I really had zero interest in proving what a jerk Nick McKelty was.

I just wanted my dog back.

My dad decided to go outside again and look on the street. He was hoping that Cheerio might have wandered into Mr. Kim's grocery store, since there's a cat named Butcher there that Cheerio likes to chase. I can't even tell you how much I was hoping the same thing.

As my dad opened the front door to leave, we heard the *ding-ding* of the elevator arriving on our floor. The doors slid open and out came Papa Pete. He was wearing a huge gray elephant head, but you could see his face through a mesh screen under the trunk. He was with Mrs. Fink, who looked exactly like—well, there's no nice way to say this—the rear end of an elephant. No disrespect intended to Mrs. Fink.

"Hello, my darling family," Papa Pete called out as he came galloping into the apartment. "Hankie, say hello to Dumbo, Part One . . ."

He swished his trunk at me like he was waving hello.

". . . And Dumbo, Part Two," he said,

gesturing to Mrs. Fink. "I'll have you know, you are looking at the second place winners in McKelty's Roll 'N Bowl Halloween Costume Extravaganza."

Papa Pete pulled out a blue ribbon from his trunk and dropped it on the coffee table. I tried to smile, but I couldn't.

"Hey, why the long face?" Papa Pete said. "I know it's not first place, but it's still pretty good. Oh, I know. You're wondering where Emily and Robert are. Well, they'll be along. They stopped off to show Robert's mother their costumes."

Papa Pete looked from me to my mom and dad. He could tell something was wrong. He pushed back his elephant head so I could see his eyes and sat down next to me.

"What's wrong?" he asked.

"Cheerio has disappeared," I said. I could hear my voice cracking as I tried to speak. "I wasn't watching him and he ran away."

"Ah, so that's what this is about," Papa Pete said.

I nodded, but I couldn't look him in the eyes. I felt bad from head to toe. Irresponsible. Ashamed. Stupid. Guilty. Sad. Take your pick, because I felt them all.

"I take it you didn't read my note," Papa Pete said to me.

"You mean the note with the instructions for the haunted house?" I asked. I wondered what that had to do with Cheerio. All I remembered about the note was that I stuffed it in my back pocket because I was too ashamed to read it out loud in front of Papa Pete.

"Yes, that note."

Papa Pete was looking at me funny. He curled the ends of his big, bushy mustache with his fingers. His mustache had gotten pretty droopy under the elephant face. It must have been hot in there. Papa Pete just sat there, rolling his mustache, waiting for me to answer.

"I . . . uh . . . didn't have time to finish it, Papa Pete. I had . . . uh . . . a lot to do."

"Can I see you on the balcony a moment, Hankie?" Papa Pete said.

I followed him out to the little balcony that is off our living room and has a peekaboo view of the lights on Broadway.

"I want you to level with me," Papa Pete said, "because I am your grandfather and I love you no matter what."

I didn't know what he was going to ask me, but I knew that whatever it was, I was going to tell the truth.

"You didn't read my note at all, did you, Hankie?"

I shook my head no.

"And why not?"

"Because . . . because I couldn't," I said. My eyes were filling up with tears. I didn't know if I was crying because I missed Cheerio so much or because I felt bad because I couldn't read Papa Pete's note or because I hadn't really told him the whole truth. All I know was that my eyeballs were very wet.

Papa Pete put his arms around me. The elephant fur of his costume smelled like peanuts.

"Talk to me, Hankie."

"There were too many words," I said, the truth suddenly pouring out in one big rush like water tumbling down Niagara Falls. "They were jumping all over the page and getting mixed up and every time I'd try to read them, I couldn't follow what they were saying. And it was on narrow-lined paper. I hate narrow-lined paper."

"Why didn't you just tell me all that?" he asked.

"Because I'm tired of always having to tell people what I can't do," I said. "It sucks. Just once, I'd like to be able to do everything that everyone else can do."

Papa Pete nodded.

"Do you still have my note?" he asked me.

I reached into my back pocket and pulled it out. It was pretty squished up, but Papa Pete smoothed it out as best he could.

"Now," said Papa Pete, pointing to a few lines at the bottom of the page. "Let's read this part together, shall we?"

He pointed to the end of the note.

"What does that say?" he asked me.

"P.S.," I said. I could read that, no problem. I even knew that's an abbreviation for something you put at the end of a letter when you've forgotten to say something in the letter. Like *P.S. I Love You* or *P.S. Longer Letter Later*.

"P.S.," I read out loud. That was a start.

"Good, Hankie. Go on. I'll help you."

"P.S. I have taken Cheerio," I read. I stopped and looked up at Papa Pete. I could feel myself starting to smile.

"Continue reading, Hankie. Follow the words with your finger if you need to. One at a time."

I pointed to each word as I read it. My eyes followed my finger, and my voice followed my eyes. The words came out . . . slowly . . . but loud and clear!

"I have taken Cheerio to Mrs. Fink's apartment so he won't get sc . . . sc . . ."

"Scared," Papa Pete read.

The words soaked into my brain.

"Papa Pete! You took Cheerio?"

"I believe that's what the note says," said Papa Pete.

I started jumping up and down like a madman. Those were the best words I had ever read!

"Let's go get him!" I screamed. "I can't wait to grab that little guy and give him an extra-special, super-duper Double-Trouble-Tummy-Ear Scratch!"

"Okay, we'll go," said Papa Pete. "But only

if you promise me one thing first."

"I know, I know," I said. "I promise that when I read out loud, I'll do it slowly and carefully. Right?"

"No, Hankie." Papa Pete took my face and held it in his big hands. He looked me right in the eyes. "I want you to promise never ever to be ashamed of who you are. Because who you are is one terrific kid, no matter how you read."

Wow. I felt like two tons of rocks had been lifted off my back.

"Papa Pete," I said, throwing my arms around him, "did anyone ever tell you that you are absolutely the best front half of an elephant in the whole wide world?"

"Actually, yes," Papa Pete laughed. "Mrs. Fink just told me that very thing."

Now I ask you—what are the odds of that???

CHAPTER 22

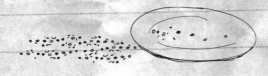

WE STEPPED BACK INSIDE our living room, grabbed Mrs. Fink, and stampeded like crazed elephants over to her place. When she opened the door, I raced inside and there he was, the cutest dog in the whole world! He was fast asleep on her shaggy gold rug, snoring like a bear. For a little dog, he has a big snore.

Man, did he look great!

"My cherry strudel," Mrs. Fink said. "I left a whole plate of it here on the coffee table. Where'd it go?"

I went over to Cheerio and scratched him gently behind the ears. He yawned and opened his eyes. When he saw me, he wagged his tail so fast, I thought he was going to take off like a helicopter.

And when he smiled, there were cherry strudel crumbs stuffed in all his teeth—bottom and top.

"I'm sorry, Mrs. Fink," I said. "He has a terrible sweet tooth."

"That's okay, darling," she said. "There's still poppy-seed Danish."

I carried Cheerio back to our apartment, and everyone was completely over-the-moon happy to see him alive and well. My mom picked him up and danced around the room. Frankie and Ashley gave him about a million pets each. Even my dad put out his hand and said, "Shake, Cheerio." Cheerio, being the nutcase that he is, didn't put his paw out to shake, but he did spin around in a circle until he fell over in a heap.

"That's our Cheerio," I said, and we all laughed.

Ding-dong.

"I bet that's McKelty," Frankie said.

I realized that was the first time I had thought about Nick McKelty since Cheerio disappeared— which just shows you how things you think are important are not so important compared to the things that are really important. You know what I mean? Good, because I'm not sure I do.

Anyway, it wasn't McKelty.

It was none other than the bacteria twins,

Emily and Robert, decked out in their finest flu-germ gear.

"So you didn't go as a princess after all," I said to Emily.

"And Robert didn't go as a knight," she answered. "You were right, Hank. We're flu germs through and through."

Then she and Robert each pulled out a trophy from behind their backs.

"We won first place!" Emily grinned, holding the trophy above her head.

"Long live the pus pockets!" Robert added.

"Everyone loved them," Papa Pete said. "But what really clinched the trophy was their interpretative dance, showing the influenza virus spreading an infection. It was phenomenal."

"Oh, that sounds so creative," my mom said. "Show us, kids."

No one had to ask them twice. Emily and Robert skipped around the room, waving their hands and pushing their stomachs out and spewing imaginary germs into the air. I'm not sure, but I think they danced (if you want to call it that) to the tune of "I'm a Little Teapot," which Emily hummed as she skipped.

I wish you could have been there. It was something to see.

I have to confess something. As I watched Emily and Robert, I did have the thought that my sister was . . . well . . . pretty weird. I mean, you'd probably think the same thing if your sister was a dancing pus pocket.

But then I realized that maybe she thought I was weird for being a table in an Italian restaurant. What's weird to one person might be normal for another person. Papa Pete's words rolled around and around in my head.

Never ever be ashamed of who you are, because who you are is one terrific kid.

Everyone in the room was smiling at Emily and Robert. My mom was clapping. My dad was tapping his toe. Papa Pete and Mrs. Fink were dancing so close, they almost looked like one whole elephant. Frankie was doing a little freestyle break dancing, and Ashley was waving Cheerio's paws around.

There we were, each being exactly who we were.

And you know what? It was really fun.

CHAPTER 23

I WOULD LIKE TO TELL YOU that I was so happy to get Cheerio back that I gave up any thought of getting even with Nick McKelty. I would like to tell you that because it would show that:

1. I had grown up and learned what was really important.
2. I had grown up and no longer needed to get even.
3. I had grown up and learned to forgive the jerk.
4. I had developed that good judgment my dad is always yapping about.

However, if I told you that any of these things were true, I would be lying. I have never lied to you before, and I'm not about to start now.

So here's the truth.

I still wanted to scare the socks off Nick

McKelty. Why? Because he was still a mean and nasty bully.

There, I've said it. Go ahead. Call me immature. I have plenty of time to get mature when I'm in the sixth grade—if that ever happens.

So after Emily and Robert had finished their dance and things had settled down, I begged my parents for permission to reopen the haunted house. There was still a chance McKelty would show up.

"You don't want to scare Cheerio," my mom warned.

"I'll watch him really closely," I said. "I promise. I've learned my lesson."

"I don't think it's a good idea," my dad said.

"I'll make you a deal, Dad," I said. "You do one more crossword puzzle and I take one more kid into the haunted house. That way, we'll both close out the evening with a bang. What do you say?"

He hesitated. I could tell he was gearing up to say no. But before he got the word out, Frankie jumped in as only he can. He and my dad have a special bond. For instance, he is the only person in the world who can get away with calling my dad Mr. Z. My dad isn't exactly the nickname type.

"Mr. Z., I have a crossword-puzzle clue for you," Frankie said. "What's a three-letter word for affirmative?"

"Yes," my dad said.

"I knew you'd say yes," I jumped in. "You got yourself a deal, Dad."

"Pretty clever, youngsters," my dad said. "Okay, Hank. You have half an hour. It's eight o'clock. If your friend isn't here by eight-thirty, we're closing up shop. Tomorrow is a school day, you know."

On that happy note, my dad went into the kitchen with my mom. Papa Pete left, too, because Mrs. Fink had a poppy-seed Danish waiting for him.

That left Frankie, Ashley, and me. Oh yes, and Emily and Robert.

"No offense, guys," I said to the bacteria twins. "But I think the flu-germ thing doesn't exactly go with the haunted house. It kind of breaks the mood."

"We want to be here to see McKelty's

reaction," Emily said. "Don't forget. He made fun of me, too."

She had a point.

"I'll make you a deal," I said. Boy, this was a big night for deal making. "You guys get rid of the pus, and we'll let you work in the haunted house."

"Really, Hank?" Emily couldn't believe her ears. Almost losing Cheerio had turned me into a total softie.

"Truthfully, I could use a little help," I said. "My number-one job from now on is to look out for Cheerio."

I figured Frankie could work the spiders. Ashley, naturally, would be the floating head. Emily could run the eyeballs, and Robert would be the brains. Robert and brains went together almost as well as Robert and mucus.

We sent Robert and Emily to change into black clothes so they wouldn't be seen, and we got the haunted house back up to speed. I went to check on the peeled grapes, but Frankie quickly took the bowl from me.

"Don't forget that I am the chief of all slimy things," he reminded me.

"How could I forget that, Frankie?"

He picked up the grapes and rolled them around in the egg whites so they were covered with a fresh coat of goo. Meanwhile, Ashley spiffed up the brains with a little extra Marshmallow Fluff. She stuck a finger in the brains.

"Yes," she said, nodding in approval. "These are definitely a ten on the ick meter."

After we straightened up the living room, rewound the tape recorder, and turned on the fan under the ghost, we squirted Ashley with some fresh ketchup. When I turned on the black light in the skeleton dude, Cheerio started to get a little jumpy. I could tell because his ears were sticking straight up in the air. I picked him up and held him in my arms.

"This is all pretend, boy," I said. "There's nothing to be scared of."

We walked over to the skeleton, and I let him take a sniff of the plastic, so he would know the bony guy wasn't real. Cheerio sniffed the leg bones and the arm bones, then licked the skeleton's ribs a whole bunch of times. This seemed pretty normal to me, because Cheerio also licks the bricks in our fireplace. He has a licking problem, I guess. But, like Dr. Berger, my educational therapist, says, we all have our issues.

"I'm ready," Emily said, coming out of her bedroom. She was dressed all in black from head to toe, including a black beanie that she had pulled down almost over her eyes. And get this. On her shoulder was—you guessed it— Katherine the Great. Emily had thrown a black washcloth over her scaly body. Katherine's, that is.

"I don't remember inviting the lizard," I said.

"Katherine would feel very left out if she weren't included," Emily answered.

"She told you that?"

"In her own way," Emily said. "We communicate nonverbally."

There wasn't time to argue, because the doorbell rang. Once. Twice. Three times.

"I bet that's McKelty," Frankie whispered.

"No, it's Robert," Emily said. "That's our special ring."

There you had it. Another fine example of

nonverbal communication at work.

Wait a minute! They have a special doorbell ring? I can't deal with this now.

Emily let Robert in. He was dressed all in black, just like Emily. Robert is so skinny that he looked like a piece of licorice I ate at the movies the Saturday before. I'm not kidding.

I checked out Frankie's watch. It was sixteen minutes after eight. We had ten minutes for McKelty to get there. Or something close to ten. You know me and numbers.

Ten minutes and counting.

CHAPTER 24

He arrived at exactly eighteen minutes after eight.

When he knocked, I cracked open the door and spoke in my lowest, raspiest voice.

"Welcome to the chamber of fear. Do you dare enter?"

"You don't scare me, Zipperbutt. I'm only here because I have nothing better to do."

That McKelty, he sure knows how to deliver a friendly greeting.

I opened the door and let him in. McKelty had added even more blood and guts to his Halloween costume, including a plastic knife sticking out of the side of his head. I was holding Cheerio in my arms because we had turned out all the lights and I didn't want him to freak out.

"You call that a dog?" McKelty said, pointing one of his beefy fingers at Cheerio. "I call it a wiener . . . without the bun."

Cheerio sniffed McKelty's finger and snarled. Then he saw the plastic knife sticking out of McKelty's head. He sniffed that, then licked it. A lot.

"Your dog is weird," McKelty said.

"He's a vampire dog," I whispered. "He loves blood. Want to let him lick you?"

Not a bad comeback, Hank. That shut him up.

I held the flashlight out in front of us and led McKelty into the living room. It was totally dark outside now, and no light came into the room except for the purple glow of the black light. McKelty tripped on the corner of the rug, lost his balance, and almost fell down. He tried to pretend it didn't happen, but I let out a crazed laugh.

"What are you laughing at, Zipweed?" he snarled.

"Lower your voice," I said. "You're making the spirits extremely angry."

From inside the haunted house, Ashley suddenly let out a bloodcurdling shriek. We hadn't even rehearsed that, but it couldn't have come at a better time. McKelty jumped three feet off the ground.

Nice touch, Ashweena!

I held the door flap open and McKelty walked in. The first thing he saw was the skeleton, glowing in the corner.

"Nick McKelty! I've been waiting to meet you," the skeleton said in a deep voice, breathing heavily. "Shake my hand."

That was Frankie, doing his Darth Vader impersonation. This wasn't rehearsed either, but again, an excellent idea.

Frankie, my man. Darth rocks!

McKelty approached the skeleton and reached for his hand. As soon as he touched it . . .

Plop! The arm fell off and rolled to the floor.

McKelty jumped four feet in the air this time. I could hear him gasp. When he saw me looking at him, he tried to act like he hadn't just done that.

"Big deal," he said to me. "It's just a fake hand."

But I saw his eye twitch.

I guided him over to the table with the grape

eyes and spaghetti brains.

"The monster Frankenstein has lost his eyes," I whispered. "He asks that you help find them."

Quickly, I grabbed McKelty's hand and pushed it into the bowl of slimy grapes Emily was holding. Just as his hand touched the grapes, Katherine let out a huge hiss. Again, unrehearsed, but another brilliant addition, if I do say so myself.

Katherine, for the first time in your whole lizardy life, fine job!

"What was that?" McKelty said, pulling his hand away from the grapes as fast as you could say "iguana breath."

"The eyes saw you," I whispered. "They're following you now."

"Those eyes are alive?" McKelty asked, his voice shaking.

"The eyes see all," Emily hissed, sounding so much like Katherine it sort of scared me, too.

Katherine hissed again and Emily joined in, then Robert. It was a regular hissfest, coming at McKelty from every direction. He backed away really fast—and as he did, he bumped into

Robert, who was holding the brains. I snatched McKelty's hand and plunged it into the goopy hat.

"Dracula's brains," I whispered in his ear. "They are alive and thinking of ways to harm you."

"Why me?" said McKelty. "I didn't do anything!" I could hear his voice cracking.

Oh, yeah. This was fun.

Then came the moment I had been waiting for!

I gave Frankie a sign, and he lowered the spiders, fast this time. They plunged down and landed smack on the back of McKelty's neck. Bull's-eye! As he turned around to bat them off, I pulled the napkin off of Ashley's blood-streaked face.

"The tarantulas!" she screamed. "They're eating my flesh!"

I thought McKelty was going to pee in his pants right there. Maybe he even did. It was too dark to see. The only thing I can tell you is that he screamed like a baby who wants his bottle.

And then, something else happened. Something unexpected. Something truly terrifying.

We heard thundering footsteps coming across the room.

Boom, boom, boom, they went.

I looked around the haunted house. We were all in there. Who could this be? Talk about unrehearsed! This was totally unexpected!

The footsteps were followed by a voice. It was soft and low, which made it even scarier.

"I vant to suck your blood!" it said. "Who will be my next victim?"

I swear to you, I was sure there was a real vampire in the room with us. I looked up, and there, peering over the top of the sheet was an actual vampire! I'm not kidding. He was tall with black slicked-back hair and a black velvet cape. His face was white and ugly. Dark red blood was dribbling out of his mouth.

He reached out his huge hand and grabbed at us. I screamed so loud, you could probably hear me from where you are now. Cheerio bolted from my arms and took off to parts unknown. Ashley and Frankie and Emily and Robert all screamed, too.

And McKelty, well, I thought he was going to collapse.

"I'm getting out of here!" he yelled. "That guy's real!"

McKelty was so panicked, he started to run in circles. When he couldn't find the door flap, he just barreled into the wall of the haunted house and brought the whole bedspread down in a heap. The vampire reached out and grabbed his collar.

"Don't suck my blood!" McKelty yelled. "Pleeasse!!!"

He wriggled free from the vampire's hand and took off, screaming down the hall. He ran into my bedroom and slammed the door. He thought it was the front door of the apartment. A second later, my bedroom door flung open and Nick the Tick ran down the front hall with his mouth wide open, trying to scream. He was so scared, no sound came out. The vampire chased him, but McKelty got out of the apartment just in time. He must have finally got his voice back, because we could hear him screaming "Don't hurt me!" all the way down the elevator.

As for me, I had only one thought. Where was Cheerio? I raced around the living room looking for him. Even if there was a bloodsucking vampire in my house, I had promised to protect Cheerio, and that's just what I was going to do.

But the vampire had beat me to it. He was bending down by the couch, trying to convince Cheerio to come out from his hiding place.

"Get away!" I shouted at the vampire. "That's my dog!"

"I don't vant to scare him," the vampire said. "I love animals. Like my cow, Olga, back in Poltava. She was good friend to me."

I knew that voice. Who else could have had a cow named Olga?

"Vlady!" I said.

He peeled off his rubber mask. The vampire face disappeared and there he was, our lovable sandwich maker.

"Yes, it's me, Hank," he said.

When Cheerio saw Vlady's face, he came scurrying out from under the couch and jumped in his lap. He loves Vlady because Vlady always gives him the leftover meat from his sandwiches.

When the kids saw it was Vlady, they all came over and gathered around.

"You were stupendous, man," Frankie said to Vlady.

"Awesome," Ashley agreed.

"Did you see McKelty run?" Emily laughed.

"He looked like a scared rabbit," Robert said. "Actually, a hare to be more precise. Hares run faster than rabbits."

We all took a minute to just enjoy the thought of McKelty screaming out of the house. Let's face it, the guy deserved it.

Then a thought occurred to me.

"Let me ask you something, Vlady," I said. "How did you know that McKelty would be here?"

"I could smell his blood," he said.

His blue eyes were twinkling again.

"Come on. Tell us the truth. How'd you know when to come?"

"Vampires don't tell their secrets."

"Vlady, enough of the kidding."

"Are you sure I am kidding?" he said.

Vlady yawned. I noticed his lips looked awfully red from the fake blood. It was fake blood, wasn't it? It had to be.

What are you saying, Hank? Of course it was.

"I am tired," he said. "Now I must go sleep in my coffin."

"Vlady, you don't really sleep in a coffin," I laughed.

"It belonged to my grandfather Boris," Vlady said.

It occurred to me that I had never seen Vlady's apartment. I was sure he didn't really have a coffin there.

I mean, he couldn't. Right?

Because there's no such thing as a vampire.

Right?

These are just weird Halloween thoughts you're having, Hank. Everyone knows there's no such thing as vampires.

Right?

Absolutely right.

Right???????

CHAPTER 25

WE NEVER GOT TO TRICK-OR-TREAT. But I'm telling you, what we got that night was sweeter than two hundred bags of Halloween candy. The picture of Nick the Tick McKelty streaking out of our apartment like his pants were on fire is a picture I'm going to hold in my mind for ever and ever. Even as I think of it right now, it makes me feel like I want to stand up and shout "yes" at the top of my lungs.

As a matter of fact, I think I will. Care to join me?

"YESSSSSSSSSSSSSSSSSSSSSSSSSSSSSS!!!!!!!"